THE
YEAR
OF
LEE

THE YEAR OF LEE

Jennifer Janell

Paperback ISBN: 979-8-9915514-1-0

Published by Words2Write Publishing
San Antonio, TX

Edited by: Khloe's Thoughts Editing
Cover design by: Make Your Mark Publishing Solutions
Interior layout by: Make Your Mark Publishing Solutions

CONTENTS

ACKNOWLEDGEMENTS

Thank you, Khloe's Thoughts Editing Services for editing and Monique Mensah for helping get another great book in readers' hands.

Special thanks to the readers who took a chance on me and the authors who encouraged and inspired me. To my family and friends, your support is always appreciated.

To those who dare to live and love on their terms. May you learn from the people you meet and moments you experience.

—Jennifer Janell

PROLOGUE

t is crazy how we make decisions or engage in behaviors that eventually cause feelings of regret and shame, even though, at the time, it didn't feel wrong or shameful at all. Is it emotion, impulse, or a twisted perspective that clouds our judgement and makes us overlook the consequences of our actions? Or do we rationalize and disguise bad habits and decisions as "indulgences" and "well-deserved pleasures"? It could be as simple as saying things we really didn't mean or as complicated as being with someone to only satisfy natural impulses and cravings. Even the most disciplined person eventually surrenders to the lure of instant gratification. Hindsight will trigger feelings of self-loathing, anger, anxiety, and the all-too-common ... regret. So, this is where I found myself, in the tangled web of situations and relationships that were not serving me well and eventually forced me to examine my "whys."

CHAPTER 1

Begin Again

Darnell's touch startled me as he grabbed my waist and dragged my body closer to his. I half-heartedly reacted with a slight lean into him. The pounding in my chest was a reminder this relationship was more than over. I wanted to scream in anger, but even more disappointed at myself for falling for his bullshit once again. Wanting to avoid another argument that could turn physical, I gave in. The way he embarrassed me at the restaurant last night was the final blow. I was done for real this time. But I had given into the alligator tears-filled apology he conjured up when we got to my place, knowing he wouldn't leave unless there was some sort of reconciliation.

My verbal acceptance of the apology wasn't enough; he wanted to have sex, believing the great fuck would make me forgive and forget. On a regular day, fucking him would have been mind-blowing because his dick game was superb.

But mentally he had messed me up so bad, there was nothing he could do to make my body respond to him.

Darnell squeezed my thigh with his large hand, a reminder of what drew me to him in the first place. He was so kind when we met eight months ago, but his tall, muscular physique was what captured me. He was built like a God with midnight colored skin. After a few conversations with him, it was evident his face belonged next to the definition of the silver tongue devil. Did that stop me from making the obvious big mistake of fucking with him? Of course not. So here I was, plotting an escape.

"Good morning, baby." His voice broke my thoughts.

"Morning," I responded.

He sighed, sensing my discontentment. "You still mad at me?"

"No, I'm okay." I lied.

"Alright then." He kissed the back of my neck; I felt the bulge against my ass, threatening another encounter.

He was trying to go for round two. I bit my lip, trying to stop myself from going off. *Damn, why are his feelings more important than mine? This is bullshit; get away from him now.* My mind was giving me a pep talk. "You should go home. I have to work tomorrow." Another lie.

"Really, Leesha? You worked last Sunday, so you should be scheduled to work next weekend." His controlling ass had memorized my work schedule.

"Yea, Mikayla texted me to cover her shift, she's sick." *He gets on my nerves.*

"Whatever, Leesha, just keep fucking lying to me."

Immediately feeling defensive, I jumped out the bed. "Are you threatening me now? You put your hands on me last night, too? Darnell, you don't know me very well at all."

"I know that you'll fuck even after being *done* so you say." He threw his hands up using air quotes as if I was a joke.

"Really? You were crying, snottin' and spittin' all over the fucking place, apologizing to me. What you got was sympathy sex and don't worry you won't be getting it anymore. Now bye, crybaby." There was my way out, no forgiving this time.

"Getting it? Getting what? You ain't all that, Leesha, with your fat ass. You light-skinned bitches think you're God's gift and ain't shit," he spewed, putting on his clothes.

"Is that all you got? Fat? Light-skinned? Newsflash, I know I'm not skinny, and I have been this color all my life. But what I will not be is disrespected by a controlling, insecure ass dude. Like I said before, bye!" I dismissed him again.

Darnell stormed out the door, slamming it. I took a deep breath and cursed myself for putting up with him that long. I was just tired of being alone when I got tied up with him. That was a huge mistake.

My friend, Mikayla, had told me to leave him alone after the first time I was with him and bragged to her about how great the dick was. She said, "If the dick is that good, you best get off it immediately. He's nothing but trouble." She was right, he didn't give me anything but a wet ass and a hard time. His insults were always masked in a joke or an off-handed comment that had slowly erased the little confidence I did have. My weight had always been a struggle, but complete insecurity about it didn't happen until I met him. He always commented on my skin color as if being biracial was an offense. I actually considered myself as Black because I never was accepted by my father or his family. My caramel skin and kinkier than straight hair was a badge of honor to me because most people did not guess I was biracial. Regrettably, I was an open book with Darnell, and he used every doubt or insecurity against me.

I was afraid he would come back around. The last encounter we had wasn't as intense as it could have been. But the night before, he humiliated me at the restaurant after I questioned him about constantly being on his phone at dinner. That asshole hit the table, told me to mind my business, and grabbed my face so hard it left my cheeks reddened and sore. The waiter rushed over, and I assured him I was fine. I quietly told Darnell the next time he touched me he would regret it, and I meant it. He was getting free with those hands, and I wasn't the type to sit around and get my ass whipped. He was revealing his true character; the character I had seen hints of early on. Now it was evident he had serious issues.

For some reason, I kept falling for the same type of man repeatedly. Men always wanted to assert their authority over me, always accusing me of seeing other people, and talking down to me. It wasn't like I missed the clues they exhibited,

I saw them clearly and recognized them from the traits my dad had. I never hung around long after that bullshit started, so my track record of long relationships was terrible. Getting men was easy, getting the right man was hard.

The next few weeks, I went apartment hunting. Rent was crazy for where I was staying, and I wanted to get closer to the northside. I had interviewed for a supervisor position at Lotus Gardens, an assistant living facility on that side of town, and was hoping I would get it. I wasn't a fan of cleaning the house all day, so something small was good. I finally found a nice two-bedroom apartment just ten minutes from where the facility was and planned to make a down payment the next day. Another step closer to manifesting my new job and hopefully a new life. In typical Leesha style I had managed to make my life harder than it had to be by working too much and letting loneliness dictate my relationships. Now it was time to be selfish and focus on what I wanted. Dating without commitment sounded like a good idea. That would give me a chance to focus on work and have a little fun when needed.

Darnell had called a few times, but I didn't answer; hearing his voice would either soften or enrage me, either way I needed to maintain a clear head and not mess with him again. He was eventually blocked after my soul was satisfied enough with his pursuit.

❦ ❦ ❦

Early Monday morning I was on the way to the bank when my cell phone rang. It was Mr. Bryan, the owner of the facility I interviewed at. My heart was going crazy when the name popped up.

"Good morning, this is Leesha Roberts," I answered.

"Ms. Roberts, this is Mr. Bryan from Lotus Gardens. How are you?"

"I'm fine, Mr. Bryan, how are you?"

"Great but let me get right to it. We are really impressed with you and believe you will be a great fit for the facility. Are you still interested in the position?"

"Yes, I am." I gave a silent thank you to God and the universe.

"Okay, come in around noon today and we can discuss pay and other particulars."

"Perfect, I will be there and thank you so much." I hung up the phone and had a quick private celebration in the car.

The meeting went better than anticipated. I negotiated a significantly higher pay than expected and had two weeks before I started. It was just enough time to move into my new place and let go of my current job. I opted to use my remaining two weeks of paid time off to pack and do a little self-care. Aside from the fear of leaving the familiarity of an inpatient unit, I was excited for a new start. After working my butt off in one of the busiest hospitals in San Antonio and going to school for my master's in healthcare administration, I finally got a supervisor position and was so ready for the challenge.

CHAPTER 2

The Move In

I looked up at the tall apartment building, feeling like this was the start of a great adventure. The new job and place were a long time coming. I grabbed the last box out of the U-Haul and headed to the elevator. The ride to the fifth floor shifted the contents of the box, making it harder to carry.

"Do you need help with that." A deep voice caught me off guard.

"Oh no, I'm fine." I tried to speed up, looking even clumsier.

"Really, you don't look fine." A tall, light-skinned man grabbed the box. "Lead the way."

"Okay, thank you." I walked down the hallway and stopped at door 518.

"What a pleasant surprise, I live right next door. Look at you; all the help you need is right here." He had a mischievous smirk on his face that made his light, golden brown eyes sparkle.

"Thank you, but hopefully I won't be bugging you too much." I couldn't help but smile back, forgetting about my sweaty, wrinkled clothes.

"You can bug me, I ain't got shit going on." He was a flirty one.

I opened the door, and he sat the box inside, eyeing the U-Haul dolly I had accidentally left in a rush to retrieve the last box. The place was filled with boxes, bags, and loose items, so we couldn't get too far past the door.

Mr. Fine Ass scanned the room. I had already secretly given him a name.

"Yea, you need me." He leaned against the doorframe. "But I can do more than move boxes." His eyes perused my body.

"I bet you can." I met his gaze and bit the side of my lip to maintain the sexual tension this man had started. He looked like trouble, but dick right next door wasn't a bad idea, as long as it was just that, and nothing to cramp my single lady lifestyle.

"I'm Johnathon by the way." He held out his hand to greet me.

"I'm Leesha, but you can call me Lee, especially since you're my new neighbor." I continued flirting.

"Well, Lee," he leaned down and whispered in my ear. "if you need me, just come get me."

My panties instantly moistened, which was a welcomed feeling because the single life wasn't serving me well. "I most definitely will come next door if I need you. Nice to meet you."

"Nice to meet you, too. See you later, Lee." Johnathon disappeared into his apartment.

His shameless flirting distracted me, but it was time to get comfortable and recover from the move. I finally took a moment to admire my cute apartment. The floor was white with swirls of grey and black to match the small island in the kitchen that separated the cooking and dining area. The shiny stainless-steel appliances gave it a classy appearance along with the silver handles on the white cabinets and drawers. The living room was a nice size, and the back wall had a sliding door that led to a patio. I could see the expressway from there along with several surrounding restaurants, which I planned to frequent. There was a curved archway leading to the small hallway where the guest bathroom and bedrooms were. The master bedroom was spacious with a separate bathroom. This place was perfect for me.

My kitchen table and living room set were being delivered tomorrow, so the plan was to get up early, move this stuff out of the way, and start unpacking. I found some sheets and put them on the mattress, which laid on top of the box spring. My laptop was set to charge, ready for a solo Netflix date. I dug out my microwave, and in desperation cooked a cup of noodles, grabbed some water, then fell asleep watching a boring documentary.

It had been two weeks since I moved in, and my place was almost put together. There were no sightings of Mr. Fine Ass since that first day, but I could hear him up early in the mornings playing music. He didn't seem to be home much in the evening; probably was out there slinging that dick with his sexy self. My job was postponed because the current supervisor took some time off and wouldn't be back for another week to train me. By now, I was in a good place but was craving some excitement.

It was time for me to have some fun without commitment, and why not start with Mr. Fine Ass next door. Honestly, I wanted to date around and fuck on my terms for a while; no boyfriend, no one taking up my time and space, but a girl had needs.

I put on some yoga pants to accentuate my ass and a V-neck shirt to show a little cleavage, grabbed a chilled bottle of Stella Rosa, and went next door. I hoped he didn't answer because I was already losing my nerves. He opened the door after the second knock.

"Well, lucky me, do you finally need me for something?" His smile and hooded bedroom eyes made me shiver.

"No, I'm good. I just never gave you a proper thank you from last time, and I wanted to give you this." I handed him the wine.

"I think I'm the one that's supposed to be bringing you wine, but come in." His apartment smelled of men's cologne mixed with the vanilla scented candle he had burning on his kitchen island.

"I hope you weren't busy and I'm not intruding."

"You're good, perfect timing, I was about to cook me some chicken alfredo. Would you like to stay for dinner."

"No, it's okay." Now I was suddenly shy.

"Really? So, what you eatin' tonight?"

"Ummm, I got some..." I wasn't quick on my feet at all.

"Girl, if you don't get comfortable and sit down while I cook! Open the wine," he insisted. Mr. Fine Ass had a little character, but I couldn't place it yet because he was so damn cute and surely that wasn't a feminine quality I just noticed, hell no.

I made myself comfortable on his brown leather sofa. He had a heavy wooden table set with a decorative glass container adorned with candles and greenery as a center piece. There was a random small, mirrored box on the corner of the table. The room was lit by a tall colorful stained-glass lamp in the corner. The thick, beige rug covered most of his living area and gave the home a cozy feel. His place was instantly welcoming, and I felt at home.

"Okay, if you insist, I'll stay." Curiosity was setting in and I wanted to know more about him anyway.

Turned out Johnathon was a great cook; the pasta and salad were delicious. We ended up talking all night. He told me about his family in Arkansas and I told him about my mom and stepdad in Louisiana. I didn't mention my biological dad, his wife, and my half-sister because that would have totally ruined the evening.

Johnathon had one sister, and his mother was a single parent like mine. The more he drank the more he opened up, but I was careful not to tell too much about myself because I didn't come there for deep conversation; I came to make him the first on my roster.

"My mom is very religious and never opened herself up to dating after my father left," he explained. "So, dating for my sister and me was very restrictive, and as you can see, I have a lot to offer and wanted to spread this love around." He laughed, displaying his straight white teeth.

"Oh, really? So, you escaped Arkansas so you can spread your love around?"

"Not necessarily. I couldn't get with the extreme religious beliefs, so it was good for me to get on my own and start new."

"Are you dating anyone now?" I inquired.

"No one serious, but I want to find the one. I need someone because I get a little lonely sometime. What about you? Do you got a man?"

"No, I'm just out of a relationship. I want to date; not looking for anything serious now."

"Oh, so you the one wanting to spread your love around?" He smiled.

"To be honest, after my ex, I don't want anything or anyone to tie me down. Everything on my terms now, and sometimes I just need my garden watered." I couldn't help but giggle.

"Your garden watered! That's funny." He laughed. "I like you, Leesha, you're good people."

"You're cool, too. I'm glad we met." The desire to seduce Johnathon surprisingly was fading away. I decided he would be a better friend than a lover.

Johnathon was a financial consultant for a credit union. He said it was just a job and he would rather be working independently. He seemed like a free spirit, and I liked that.

I told him about my old and new job and how I loved being a nurse but wanted to make a difference for nurses and our work environment, which was why I took the job as a supervisor at Lotus Gardens. We talked about how the need for a change in scenery and acceptance into nursing school brought me to San Antonio six years ago. Our night continued with finishing off the wine and talking about hobbies and bucket lists.

I made it home about 10:30 that night. I really liked Johnathon. He was easy to talk to, funny, and easy on the eyes. I rarely considered associating with anyone on the regular. I was not the type to have a lot of friends, male or female, but this may be a welcomed change.

The next morning, I finished unpacking the last few boxes and putting everything in place. I was exhausted and decided to order some food. Instead of selecting a meal, social media hypnotized me into a semi-deep sleep. Startled by a knock on the door, I looked through the peep hole to see Johnathon holding up a bag.

"You like Mexican food?" He knew a way to a woman's heart.

"What kind of question is that? I'm starving, come in!"

He came in and opened the bags as I grabbed some extra napkins. "Do we need drinks?" I asked.

"Of course not." He presented me with a large frozen margarita.

"Oh, shit! You trynna marry me!" I yelled. We burst out laughing.

We decided to eat our food in the living room. Johnathon quickly made himself at home kicking off his shoes and stretching out on the couch and I snuggled into the loveseat. The TV was background noise to our effortless conversation. Being with him felt like hanging with an old friend, the connection was strangely comforting. It was like God knew I needed someone like him in my life.

"So, Lee, besides just getting out of a bad relationship, why don't you have some damn back-ups sniffin' around? I mean you a pretty girl, so what's up?" he inquired.

"Shit, San Antonio is not really a good spot to be single. When you finally find a dude that is single, got a half-way decent job, mentally stable, look like somethin' then you gotta worry about if he gay or not. These men be out here lookin' for the same shit I'm lookin' for." I took a sip of my margarita. "Plus, I can't keep em' long anyway, not even a year. Either they're crazy, or I'm in my head and start actin' crazy," I admitted.

"Oh, so you worried about competing with the gay dudes, huh?" Johnathon turned serious, which threw me off because this wasn't a serious conversation.

"Amongst other things." I matched the energy. "Not saying it bothers me, it's just a fact."

"Got it." He managed a fake laugh and rubbed his eyes. He put his plate down like he had lost his appetite.

"I didn't offend you, did I?" My stomach ached and I shivered at the sudden change in the air.

"No, I'm not offended." He took a deep breath. "I guess I should tell you that I'm bisexual, I mean before you go off on an 'all these gay Black men' rant, that I have heard far too many times." He continued staring at the floor.

"No, Johnathon, I have never felt the need to rant about gay Black men, and I'm perfectly fine with you being bisexual, gay, straight, I really don't care. Now, you fine as hell and I did have plans for you before I really got to know you." I giggled.

"Oh really." He grinned.

"You're so fun and real and I need that right now. Anyway, you're filed in the friend category because I ain't about to risk losing that; I told you I can fuck up a relationship quick." I offered a reassuring smile.

"You're so funny." He chuckled.

"I mean, what more could I ask for, a neighbor that feeds me and has good conversation!"

"Right!" Johnathon looked relieved. "I didn't want to lose this either, it's nice to have someone to talk to right next door," he admitted.

After confession time was over, we had another great evening eating and drinking. One thing I noticed was he really liked his cocktails. That was okay because so did I, but I couldn't be doing this regularly with my new job.

CHAPTER 3

The New Job

I t actually took a month for me to finally start the new job. I was anxious to start, but kind of sad to get serious after spending almost every evening hanging with Johnathon. I arrived at Lotus Gardens just before 7:30 a.m. to start orientation with the outgoing supervisor, Mr. Van. There was an older woman with silver hair sitting at the front desk. She did not acknowledge me when I walked up. She didn't even look up and I could tell she knew I was there.

"Excuse me, good morning. I'm Ms. Roberts here for Mr. Van," I spoke.

"Yea, sign in." She motioned toward a tattered book sitting on the counter, still ignoring my presence. It appeared to be a visitor's log.

"Is this a visitor sign in? Because I'm not a visitor, I'm a new employee." I kept a smile glued to my face, trying to break her icy wall.

"Oh okay, I'll call Mr. Van." She picked up the phone. "Yes, Mr. Van there's a new employee here for you. Her name is umm..."

"Ms. Roberts," I reminded her.

"Yes, Ms. Roberts. Okay thank you." She hung up the phone. "He will be right out."

"Thank you," I said. Once again, no response from this lady. I hoped every visitor wasn't treated like me. This was something to address once settled into my position. Five minutes went by, and she seemed irritated that Mr. Van had not showed up and I was still standing there.

"Welp he's not here yet of course. Probably walking around doing nothing," she scoffed. This was too unprofessional for me, considering I was new. She was already trying to leave me with negative vibes.

"It's okay. I'm sure he's busy and will be here shortly." I remained calm.

"Yea, right." She continued typing.

A tall, white man with a bald head appeared around the corner. "Ms. Roberts, I'm Mr. Van. You can call me Todd."

"Hello, nice to meet you. Please call me Leesha." I shook his hand.

"Leesha, nice to meet you, too. I see you have met Mary, our receptionist. Mary, this is Leesha Roberts, she is the one taking over when I leave. She will be running the show."

Mary's eyes darted up, finally making eye contact with me. "Oh, oh...well hello." She shook my hand.

"Hi," I responded. "How long have you been here?"

"Six years," she answered.

"Great, we'll talk soon." I gave her that 'I got your ass now' grin and followed Mr. Van to the office area.

Mr. Van took me down a back hallway that led to double glass doors. There was a young lady with short red hair and emerald eyes sitting at a desk.

"Beth, this is Ms. Roberts. I'll be training her as my replacement." He introduced us.

"Hello, Ms. Roberts. I will be your secretary." Her smile was genuine.

"Hello." I was grateful to have a nice person in that position, especially since I would probably be leaning on her for a lot.

We walked through some wooden double doors, which revealed a big office that housed two fully furnished desk areas. A medium built, handsome Hispanic man with dark hair and light eyes was sitting at the desk in the far-left corner.

"You must be Ms. Roberts." He jumped up. "I'm your assistant, Daniel."

"Great! I definitely need you! How long have you been here?" I asked.

"Ten years, me and Mr. Van got here the same time." He shook my hand.

"Awesome. Glad to have such experience here." I wondered why he didn't take this position, but that would be a conversation for another day.

"Oh, I'm very glad you are here," he said with a slightly raised eyebrow. That look on his face had a story behind it.

"Let me take you on a tour of the facility," Mr. Van interrupted.

"Great. Mr. Bryan gave me a quick tour, but I really didn't have time to take everything in."

Mr. Van gave me an extensive tour. The Black employees looked a little surprised but were friendly. The younger white employees were really nice and the older white ones had a "what the hell" look followed by a fake hello. One lady, Nancy, stood out to me. She made no efforts to at least pretend to like me.

"And what's your name again?" she started drilling me.

"Ms. Roberts."

"Oh, so you are our new supervisor, but know nothing about working here. Go figure, another bad choice by our fearless superiors. No offense, I'm just saying, we need someone that knows this place." She glanced at Mr. Van then turned her back on him in an act of blatant disrespect.

"No offense taken. Did you interview for the position? Seems like you have a strong opinion of how this place should run." I was sure to maintain a neutral expression.

"Well, we never even knew the position was opening. I'm not the only one who would have been better for that position; there are a few of us who have been here a while and would've loved the opportunity. But we are always disregarded." Her callous words were obviously intended for Mr. Van, but I decided to cut this little interaction short.

"Well, I am open to any suggestions that will make Lotus Gardens the best it can be, and it's always good to have people that are passionate about improvement. I look forward to working with you." I held out my hand for Nancy to shake and she just looked at it.

"Oh no, you want this mess, you got it. I'm just coming to work, doing my job, and leaving. I ain't got time to be helping someone already paid to know it all." Her ill-chosen comments persisted.

"It's always better to be part of the process and solution, instead of being part of the problem; most would agree on that." I stood taller and made direct eye contact with her. The smirk on her face was an unofficial challenge to war. I tried to shake that encounter off, but my chest ached and body grew hot. I wondered how many people Nancy represented because there was no way the boldness she demonstrated had been unsupported by others.

My hands were going to be full, and apprehension was creeping up in me. In this profession, success depended on the relationship with the staff. Insecurity and anxiety challenged the confidence I had when I first walked through the doors of Lotus Gardens.

CHAPTER 4

Just Friends

t was 7:30 p.m. and I hadn't heard from Johnathon. We had agreed to watch a movie that was premiering on Netflix. I knocked on the door and was met with a disheveled, teary Johnathon.

"Johnathon, what is wrong? What happened? Are you okay?" My barrage of questions did not allow him to answer. He just shook his head as the tears flowed down his face.

"Lee, it's not a good time, I…I can't deal with anyone else today. I… just want to be alone," he stuttered.

"There is no way I'm leaving you like this. What happened?" I squeezed through the door as he half-heartedly tried to close it. "Johnathon, I know you are upset, but I am here for you, so talk to me."

He took a deep breath, grabbed a paper towel, and dried his tears. "This asshole, Charles, at work…was making these fucked up comments and I didn't know what the hell was going on. We were in a meeting and every time I spoke, he would start interrupting me, talking over me and shit. Then finally I shut his ass down. Told him, *'when I'm done talking, you can have the floor.'* Then he said for me to quit acting like a bitch and let others talk. Me… a bitch? Lee, so this shit was pissing me off. I stood up and said, *'I don't know where all this is coming from but let's just keep it professional and stay on task.'* He kept fucking talking and basically started making comments about what he thinks he knows about my private life, and I finally lost it. I told him I would whip his little ass if he kept talking shit to me. We were in each other's face going at it." Johnathon was now pacing back and forth.

"I can't believe it, but why?" I was confused.

"First off, I know Charles' brother, and he is gay, we know some of the same people but that is all, no crazy shit, I just know that circle. I ain't out here like that, I stay to myself because of stupid shit like this. Second, that promotion I got, well I guess he thought he deserved it more. Then he said there was no telling what I did to get promoted. The other associates, Zia and Rosalyn just sat there looking stunned and I'm just as shocked, but more mad than anything. Anyway, we got into it and Mr. Taylor came in and broke it up. Everyone went back to their desk and Mr. Taylor called Charles into the office. The door was closed so I couldn't ear hustle like I wanted to. Then Mr. Taylor calls me into the office. So, I go to shut the door, and he says to leave it open. This motherfucker, acting like I'm going to do something to him. I don't know what; try to fuck him because I'm bi or beat his ass because I'm Black?"

"What did he say?" I asked, still trying to make sense of this.

"Just apologized for Charles' behavior and told me I'm great at my job, and he hopes this does not affect my work. He assured me that Charles would be dealt with appropriately. But Leesha, why couldn't I shut the door? I know he thinks the same shit about me." Johnathon was now opening a bottle of Patrón. He poured two shots and handed me one.

"Johnathon, I don't think he feels that way about you. Mr. Taylor was the one who recommended you for the promotion, so he thinks highly of you." I tried to reassure him. But he just shook his head and turned on some music.

"I feel like that whole scene made everyone look at me differently. All the interactions I had after that confrontation felt weird. Maybe I'm just too in my head, but I work hard for my reputation, and this is just sad. I feel like never going back to that fucking place." Johnathon covered his face and all I could do was hug him.

After three more shots my head was floating. Soon Johnathon pulled out the mirrored box, opened it, and laid out some papers. He had smoked before in front of me, but I never indulged. He carefully rolled a joint, lit it, and took a long drag.

"Here," he offered it to me like many times before. This time I took it. He stared at me as I inhaled and slowly exhaled, letting the smoke escape into a steady stream. His hooded bedroom eyes sparkled. I passed it back and continued soothing his hurt ego.

"I'm sorry that happened to you." I gave him another hug. "Not everyone knows what a beautiful person you are." He laid his head in my lap; eyes watery clearly still upset. "Hey, let me run you a bath and cook for you," I offered.

"Oh shit, you want to cook? Shit is getting worse." He managed a little laugh.

"Really, just because you're a Master Chef, doesn't mean you can't eat my food. I'm trying to be nice to you, boy!"

I ran Johnathon a warm bath with Epsom salt, lavender bubble bath, and lit some candles to relax him even more. He got into the tub while I searched the kitchen for something quick to cook. I put some chicken tenders in water to thaw and peeked in on him. He was just sitting there staring into space. I sat on the edge of the tub, grabbed his towel, and squeezed the warm water down the back of his neck. He closed his eyes, took a deep breath, and laid his head on my thigh. I took my slippers off and sat on the top of the tub behind his head resting my feet in the water. After lathering my hands with the lavender soap to massage his neck and shoulders, he rested his head against my stomach. Johnathon scooped up some water and returned the favor by massaging my thigh. My lounging dress allowed his hands to glide freely. I adjusted my dress to maintain my modesty. Johnathon continued rubbing my legs, then gave me chills when he softly kissed my right inner thigh. I rubbed his neck, then leaned down and gently kissed the top of his head. He looked up and touched my face, leaned in, and gave me a lingering kiss. I hungrily succumbed to his soft lips. He then turned to kiss my left thigh, and I was slowly melting. This was my friend, and I knew I was asking for trouble by reciprocating his advances, but rejection was the last thing he needed. Johnathon turned toward me and lifted himself to devour my lips once more. I glided my hands down his back, and his body felt as fascinating as I'd always imagined. He stood up, grabbed the towel, covered his dick, took my hand, and led me to his room. My heart was beating with nervousness, fear, and excitement. When we got to his room his eyes captured mine again as he leaned in and gave me another breathtaking kiss.

"You scared?" His voice was low.

"Yes." I tried to hide my nerves with a light laugh.

"Don't be. You know I will always take care of you."

Trusting him, I peeled my dress off and slipped out of my panties as he reached in his top drawer and grabbed a condom. I slid into the bed, and he got in next to me immediately caressing my face.

"If you don't want to, just say so."

"I want to," I confessed.

He hugged me and proceeded to kiss every inch of me. I felt like I was having an out of body experience but had the pleasure of being completely present at the same time. I was floating as Johnathon took his time. He finally entered me sending a slow shockwave through my body. My already wet pussy flooded, allowing him to slide in easily. Johnathon's long, thick dick massaged my walls, triggering me to tremble. The tension left as our souls slowly drifted up and intertwined in a spiritual dance above our physical bodies. My hands glided across his back as he slowly brought me to ecstasy. We came, transforming our friendship into something more complicated.

I woke up with Johnathon still holding me. My head was throbbing from the alcohol and weed. *What am I doing? I must be crazy. My best friend? But this man feels so good, so amazing.* My thoughts were interrupted when Johnathon spoke.

"Good morning, Lee."

"Good morning, Johnathon."

"We fucked up, didn't we?" he whispered.

"I don't know, but I think so." I became more confused as he squeezed me tighter. "I should go."

"You should." Johnathon didn't release his grip.

After a few more minutes, he got up and went to the bathroom. I took the opportunity to throw on my clothes.

"You just leaving without saying bye?" His voice startled me.

"No, I was going to wait."

"Yeah, right. So did last night scare you off?" He avoided my eyes.

"Nothing will scare me off from you, but I'm a little confused right now."

"I know, me too, but we can admit that we are better off as friends. If we fucked around for real, that would be the most toxic shit ever." His words stung, but they were true. "Don't get me wrong, I could stay between those legs all day. Shit, now I know that's my fuckin' happy place because it's you, and our energy is so fuckin' powerful. I can't explain it." He took the words out of my mouth.

"You don't have to. I felt it, too," I admitted.

"Yea, but you are the best friend I never had. Chances are, if we mess around and keep doing this, feelings will be hurt, and I don't want to risk losing you. Understand?" Johnathon was serious, leaving me to deal with any feelings I may have accidentally caught.

"Yeah, I do. I have to go," I said, rushing to the door.

A wave of relief hit me as I entered my apartment. Last night fucked with my head so bad. My pussy was throbbing because… shit I wanted to go back for more, and my heart was breaking because he was right about us being better as friends. Anyway, he had a bad day and shit just happened. He and I crossed a line that we shouldn't have. Alcohol, raw feelings, and sex—the whole scene was wrong. But it was Johnathon, so I couldn't be angry or avoid him like I would do anyone else. My loneliness made it easy for me to give in to him.

Johnathon had been on my mind all day, and eventually made his way to my dreams that night. In the dream we were walking down the street holding hands, laughing, and talking. It felt so right. Then we got to a street called Eternity Lane. There was only one gorgeous house surrounded by a black decorative fence on that street. When it was time to go in, Johnathon stopped.

"Leesha, I'm not supposed to go in with you."

"But why? Don't be silly, this is Eternity Lane, you have to come with me," I insisted.

"No sweetheart, I can't. This place is for you, not me." Johnathon leaned in to kiss me but faded away before our lips connected.

That dream shook me and my heart was going crazy. What did it mean? I grabbed a notebook and wrote it down, hoping to get clarity later.

Johnathon and I went on with our days acting like nothing happened. There was still a few fleeting moments that could have dragged us back to that intimate place. But with us intimacy was more than physical, the way we related to each other, looked at each other was a comfortable familiarity I had never experienced. It was inevitable we had another accidental rendezvous. The connection seemed stronger than our first encounter, but once again we were under the influence. My goal was to have a selfish, carefree time and have some good sex while I was at it. My year of selfish relationships was not going as planned. Johnathon was the one that could make me lose control with the combination of a great friendship, emotion-filled sex, followed by the "just forever friends" lecture. I felt used, but not enough to stop hanging out with him. I vowed to take the sex out of our equation because I wanted a good friendship more than anything. That was what I needed.

CHAPTER 5

Meeting Mike

"Good morning, can I get a small coffee with an extra shot of espresso please?" That was my regular order at the local coffee shop.

"Okay, Lee, how's your morning going?" Kim asked.

"Good, I guess. How's yours? You're busy today." I observed the full tables.

"Yes, I'm so grateful we're finally picking back up. It's hard competing with these franchise coffee shops.

"Right, the only businesses being built are coffee shops, car washes, and vape shops; it's crazy," I said.

"Well, there's that new office building up the street with that popular law firm in it. I've gotten a few regulars from them. There is this nice-looking guy that stops by every day; just eye candy though, he's married." Kim looked up and there was a glimmer in her eye. "Speak of the devil, there he is."

I turned for a quick glance, but the handsome man was already staring at me, causing our eyes to lock. He stood behind me as Kim turned away to finish my order. I was uncomfortable with him so close. The aroma of a masculine but sweet cologne filled my nose. Kim turned around, peeping the discomfort on my face.

"Here you go, Lee. You need anything else?" She smirked and lifted her eyebrow.

"Umm, yea can I get a cream cheese croissant." My nervousness was turning into irritation. *Did this man know anything about personal space?*

"That will be $7.89," Kim said.

"Got it." His voice sent a chill up my spine as he reached around and threw ten dollars on the counter. Her smirked widened into a full smile.

I grabbed my order and turned around. "Thank you, if I'd known you was buying, I would've gotten two." I gave a little wink and walked away. I felt his eyes follow me, so I made sure to put an extra bounce in my step.

That stranger stayed on my mind all day. He was tall, chocolate, well-groomed mustache, and beard, and not to mention he smelled like I could lay on that chest all night. I remembered Kim had told me he was married so I stopped with the fantasy. Hopefully I wouldn't see him again. I was a little late today so maybe that was his regular time.

Daniel and I slacked off that day because staffing was good, and all complaints had been addressed. I was four months in and still trying to navigate this new position, but I did have some easy days. After six weeks of training with Mr. Van, he was more than excited to leave, but I was barely ready to fly on my own. Daniel had to hold my hand and dry some tears, but I persevered. Today, we spent our time chatting and snacking. I knew I needed to slow down on eating because all my clothes were getting snug, but I didn't care. I deserved some indulgence.

"So how are you liking it so far?" he asked.

"I'm not sure yet. Seems like some staff are not too fond of me. I don't think they like newbies coming in and supervising them. I feel like I have a target on my back." I had been waiting to have this conversation with Daniel.

"It's not just a newbie that they don't like. I know who you are talking about, and those ladies don't like anyone supervising them, whether it's a new person or someone that has been here for a long time. They're just miserable and take everything out on whoever, even their coworkers on the floor."

"That's not good. Is that why you didn't take this position? I'm sure you're more than qualified." I finally got a chance to ask that burning question.

"Honestly, I've watched Mr. Van deal with those hateful bitches for years. This is my second career and I'm too damn old to be stressed out like that. Also, there's a lot of shit he didn't address. I tried to do what I could, but I needed him to back me on things, and he was just too weak to come through, so I gave up. Besides, me and my wife are doing a lot of projects around the house, and I want to focus on those." Daniel divulged more than I thought he would.

"Interesting... I guess we need to talk about what you tried to do and what changes you think will be good for this place. I have my own list as well," I suggested.

"Yeah, let's take some time tomorrow for that and keep relaxing today; I'm enjoying this. I appreciate the fact that you come in every morning and address everything right away, even if it involves having tough conversations with people. I'm used to Mr. Van leaving that all to me and procrastinating on difficult issues. This is a nice break."

"I'm just trying to get to know the staff and want them to know me. How are they going to come to me with concerns if there is no relationship or standards set?"

"True, I must say, I like your style. Things will get hard, but I know you'll be able to handle it," he reassured me.

"Things are already hard, but I'll keep going." I had said all the right things, but deep down, doubted I would last till the next month. There was a group of old disgruntled women dead set on running me out of there. Honestly, they were winning.

I was unusually tired despite going to bed earlier than normal. I had dreamed about the coffee shop man, which was weird to me because I rarely had pleasant dreams and didn't even know him. The attempt to shake off thoughts of this man was futile. He was no different than any other nice-looking man on the street, so I hoped to get him off my mind.

In an effort to avoid Mr. Coffee I left earlier, but as soon as I got out of my car, I caught a glimpse of him going through the door. *Shit, I can just get back in the car and wait for him to leave.* Who was I fooling? The attention whore in me decided to go in. As soon as I walked in, I spotted him sitting at the table nearest to the door.

"I got you two." His voice was deep and enticing.

"Excuse me?"

"Two cream cheese croissants and a coffee with a shot of espresso. Ain't that what you get?" He licked his lips, triggering a tingle down below.

"I usually get one," I responded while trying to smooth my hair back, now overly conscious of my appearance.

"But I paid, so it's two, right? Have a seat." He gestured toward the empty seat across from him.

"You really didn't have to, I was just kidding yesterday," I said, sitting down. "How'd you know what kind of coffee I get?"

"Kim, of course." His laugh was just as smooth as he was. "What's your name?"

"Leesha. What's yours?"

"Michael Sinclair, pleasure meeting you." He held out his hand.

"Pleasure is mine, Mr. Sinclair, and thank you for breakfast." *Look at me…already weak*, I thought.

"Please call me Mike. That's not really a good breakfast, but you're welcome. So, you're a nurse or something?" he asked, looking at my way too snug scrubs.

"Yes, I just took a position up the street at Lotus Gardens."

"Well, go ahead then! Congratulations on your new job." His sexy smile sent a swarm of butterflies to my stomach.

"Thank you." I couldn't stop smiling back. "What about you? What do you do?"

"I'm a lawyer with the firm that opened in that new building up the way."

"Interesting." I took a sip of coffee. His eyes were fixed on me again in another unbreakable gaze. He picked up his coffee and the gold band with three big diamonds reminded me why I shouldn't have been sitting there. "Well, thanks again. I have to go now; it was nice chatting with you." I got up, pushed my chair in, and walked away. Once again, those eyes followed me.

It seemed like every other day I ran into Mike a.k.a Mr. Coffee. Truth be told I was actually starting to look for him. The mental fight to avoid a crush on this man was difficult; my belly did a little flip every time I saw him. He did something to me every time he smiled my way and continued with relentless, shameless flirting. It sounded terrible but I had secretly talked myself into saying yes if he ever offered a little rendezvous. I really didn't want shit but to have some fun, it was time for me to be selfish for once. I needed to let loose and worry about my needs. Now it was all about me and no apologies this time. The fateful day came when Mike took the flirting a step further.

"Hey, Leesha. Why don't you have a drink with me; I mean a real drink, not coffee."

"Oh really, where do married men go have drinks with other women?" I continued to play hard-to-get.

"Touché, touché. I apologize; I was out of line for even asking." He backed away.

"I guess, ain't nothing wrong with asking for what you want," I said matter-of-factly.

His eyes darted up and peered at me. "I'm definitely a man that knows what he wants."

"Yes, you want a drink. At least that's all you asked for. There's no harm in having a drink, I guess." I made sure my eyes said the words my lips didn't. He caught on quickly.

"Well, you just made my day. Can we meet up tonight? There's a small bar on the corner."

"Or… you can come to my place." My risky offer surprised him.

"You sure about that, Ms. Leesha?" His shocked expression made me laugh.

"I'm sure. Nothing is going down, but some drinks, I promise."

We exchanged numbers and I gave him my address. I was reckless and knew it wasn't going to be good.

That evening, I chatted with Johnathon on the phone for a while. He was going out but didn't disclose where. I told him a friend was coming over and he didn't ask for details. The promise of just having a drink was becoming more laughable as I started getting ready for Mike's visit. I took a good shower, did a touch up shave, and made sure my body was primed and ready for whatever. The casual black halter top dress was also purposely revealing. I sat and waited for him, attempting to have another come to Jesus talk with myself about why this man should not even step foot in my place, but the selfish part of me continued to rationalize it.

Mike knocked on the door for a while before I opened it. He smelled amazing and looked even better.

"Wow, I can't believe your wife let you out the house looking so good?" I teased.

"Yea." My comment obviously annoyed him. "We both know I'm married, and we both know it was you that invited me over. So no need for the reminders either way, right?" His bluntness made my excitement dwindle. There was that gut feeling warning me again, letting me know I was messing with fire. He must've read the expression on my face. "What I'm saying is let's just chill and focus on the here and now. Let's relax, we both had a long week. I'm sorry, it was a rough day at the office." He walked in, removing his jacket.

"Okay, understood, but you need to understand that I will make any comment I want in my home, so trying to shut me down, regardless of how innocent it is, won't go well for you." I was direct, letting him know I wasn't feeling that asshole attitude he walked in with.

"I apologize. I guess my mind is still in work mode and sometimes I have to talk shit to get my point across. Those white boys always testing me like I didn't go to law school just like they did." His voice was lined with frustration.

"Oh, I get it. Sit down and get comfortable. What you drinkin'?"

"Anything you got, but preferably somethin' brown."

"Got you." I poured two glasses of Crown and Coke, mostly Crown for him.

We drank, talked, laughed, and listened to R&B love songs, setting a dangerous mood. There was a brief conversation about his wife, nothing bad. Matter of fact, it was obvious he loved her and had no plans of leaving. That was good because the less commitment risk, the better.

"That new law firm is driving me crazy. They always try to bust my balls every time I open my mouth. I have to stay ten feet ahead of them, just to keep up. My wife ain't tryin' to hear me complaining about work. Her father gave me a job at his law firm, but I had to get from under him; he wanted to run the firm and my household; always had an opinion on shit that wasn't any of his business. So now, every time I comment about my job, she comes with *'you should have stayed with my dad's firm,'* and I'm tired of hearing that shit," he confessed.

"I'm sure she wants the best for you; why struggle trying to keep up with the new firm when you can easily work with good ol' father-in-law." I took a sip of my drink, already feeling faded.

"I need to be the man of my own house, that's it. So, the communication is strained between me and my wife right now."

"That's unfortunate." I didn't have much to say about his situation.

Finally, he announced he had to go. We were standing by the door, and I didn't remember exactly what we said but he suddenly caught me off guard and gave me a tongue-filled kiss. My overly relaxed muscles leaned into him and my mouth fell into the rhythm of his. His hands massaged the back of my head, then down my back, relaxing me even more. Next thing I knew, we were against the wall in the hallway next to my bedroom. He ended up fucking me so good, I knew I was in trouble.

Mike got what he came for that night, filling me with a combination of regret and a hunger for more. Not to mention… the guilt. But did that stop me? No, I had lost my footing because the time we spent together was nice. Now I was willing to keep doing it. I had descended into yet another toxic situation. My head claimed I would not be seeing him again, but my body knew otherwise.

A few nights later he stopped by, but nothing happened. I played harder to get using the 'I don't sleep with married men' routine. I didn't even convince myself, much less him. He laughed and said, "okay." During that visit, we just talked and flirted a bit.

The next week he stopped by, clearly upset about something. But he calmed down as soon as he got comfortable on my couch, pulled me closer, and kissed me. I pulled away, continuing my innocent role. He paired his phone to my Alexa and played some music, which was getting me in the mood. I was in the kitchen refreshing our drinks when *Lifetime* by Maxwell came on. He came behind me and held me tight as we swayed to the music. I turned toward him, burying my head into his chest, and dared to close my eyes. It felt like that was where I was supposed to be. This song resonated with us and that moment scared me because just for a second, I wanted Mike to be mine, and only mine.

Mike sensed the shift and gave me a gentle kiss, the taste of liquor gradually intoxicating me, urging me to fall under the spell he was slowly casting. Passion crept in as he lifted me up and sat me on the kitchen island. I closed my eyes as he took gentle control of my body. He exhaled as I caressed his head, and he teased my breasts. His hands were under my dress, exploring my curves and teasing my pussy. We moaned as he pushed my panties to the side and hungrily kissed and licked my breasts, then back up to my lips, swiftly entering me, sending a sensual ache through my body. His dick moved in and out, soothing my painful desire for him. I rolled my hips, encouraging him to keep going. He strengthened his grip trying to force me to stop.

"Oh fuck, oh fuck, stop baby, you drivin' me fucking crazy," he pleaded. My ample hips weren't easy to tame; I managed a few more grinds before I came. I wrapped my legs tightly around him and he carried me to the room where we continued. He turned me around, pleasuring me from the back slightly more aggressive now. Then he turned me to the side, rubbing my pussy, releasing my wetness. He entered me one more time, making me cum again, then he finally came.

"Damn, Lee, you are so fuckin' addictive. I think I'm in trouble, shit!" he said, covering his face. I studied his body, only his dick covered with the sheet, exposing his broad chest and long muscular legs as he laid there like a model. I was the one in trouble. This man did not disappoint, and I craved him now, not just physically but mentally.

CHAPTER 6

Winning Lotus

Settling into this new position was difficult. Many of the nurses had been there for years and had no plans to take a higher position but had a lot of interest in running everything. There was strong opposition to any suggestions I made or any changes implemented. Daniel suggested we leave work and have lunch at a nearby restaurant.

"I see this position is stressing you out. You need to know you are the best person to handle this mess." He started with a pep talk.

"I feel like I'm drowning, and certain nurses are sabotaging everything that would improve that place. It's something about me that they hated as soon as I walked through the door. It's just fuckin' crazy." I knew it was most likely my race, considering the type of nurses that were giving me problems. I wanted to hear Daniel say it, so I wouldn't feel so crazy.

"Right, those ladies never liked anyone new to come in and have authority. Listen, I'll be straight with you. You got an old ass white nurse, and an old Hispanic one; you are a younger Black woman, who walked in and has been asked to run the show. They hate that shit." Daniel finally confirmed what I thought.

"I figured race had something to do with it, but this shit is so sad." I was more frustrated than before.

"Listen, you need to get the rest of the staff on your side. Don't let a few nurses speak for you. Have some meetings, three on the day shift and three on the night shift, and don't forget the weekend staff. Offer the staff a chance to discuss issues that are important to them or what they would like to see changed. Then tell them your vision and what you have observed. Let them get to know you and once again extend your open-door policy. You're going to have to put yourself out there and ignore the negativity." Daniel's suggestions were good, but I still felt defeated.

The next day, I carefully selected the meeting dates and times. A mass email was sent out for the mandatory meeting. The promise of food helped decrease some of the irritated grumbles from the staff. The email also included the agenda, so they could prepare to participate and voice their concerns in the meeting.

The first meeting was on a Monday morning. I got there early to set up. I covered the table with a purple tablecloth, a playoff of the Lotus Garden logo, and put tacos, donuts, kolaches, and fresh fruit out. There were bottled waters, apple juice, orange juice, and coffee with a variety of creamers. Next to the sign in sheet there was a box with pens, lanyards, and small hand sanitizers for the staff to take. Half the staff came while the other half worked.

"Wow, thank you, Ms. Roberts. No one has ever had a meeting with all the goodies!" they said, showing appreciation. The staff consisted of nurses, aids, housekeeping, dietary, maintenance, and others from the transportation and extracurricular staff.

"You are very welcome. You all deserve it. Thank you for coming." I felt optimistic.

Everyone filled their plates and cups before finding a seat then I started the meeting.

"Good morning and thanks again for coming. For those of you who have not met me, I'm Leesha Roberts, the new supervisor for Lotus. I wanted to have a meeting with you all to not only talk about my expectations but to listen to what you think can be improved and how those improvements can be made. To be transparent, this is not a gripe session but a meeting of the minds to discuss these pressing issues." I was met with mostly head nods, but there were also a few eye rolls, which made it easy to identify the negative ones in the group.

"Ms. Roberts, have you ever run a place like this? Seems like you don't know what you're doing." Of course, one of the negative ones started. It was Nancy who felt the need to take this in a bad direction. It was time for me to show my professionalism and not feed into her attack.

"I've had experience in leadership positions, but have never had the pleasure of working in an environment such as Lotus. With my experience I do bring a lot to the table, and it is apparent that a positive change here is necessary. Can you please give me an example of what I have done to make it appear to you that I don't know what I'm doing? I would love to hear your feedback." I opened the floor to Nancy again. The other staff members looked back and forth between me and her.

Nancy's lips pursed shut and she rolled her eyes. "Well, some changes make no sense." Her voice was especially annoying today.

"Such as?"

"Well, a lot of things. We all talk about it." She looked to her co-workers for help.

"Really? Give me an example, please." I continued looking at her, obviously this was between us because everyone else was staying out of it.

"All the extra duties you gave to the charge nurses. We gotta do too many things and you added checking the assistant living residents every day. It's hard to do a face-to-face check with everyone and do our other duties. There are other nurses and aids that see them every day. If you don't trust them to tell us if something is wrong, they're the ones that need all the extras, not adding to our already full plates," she ranted.

"I'm not asking you knock on every door; most of them you can see at mealtime in one room. I'm asking that you do lay eyes on the assistant living residents; they are here because they do need extra help and as a charge for that day if you do not see a resident out and about, you do need to check on them. I do trust the staff here to relay important information, but people are placed here for medical needs, and we need to be vigilant about meeting their medical and personal needs. There were reports of some residents being ill or hurt and were not found until a bathing aid came almost twenty-four hours later. That is dangerous and quite frankly, negligent. So, everyone should do their part. What are the other concerns or changes that make no sense to you?"

"Never mind, it don't matter no way, you're just gonna do whatever and no one's gonna say anything." She threw her hands up with a disgusted look etched on her already hardened face.

"The floor is open for anyone. If there are changes I have made that truly affect this facility in a negative way, I would like to know. One caveat to that, with the *concern* or *complaints* about the changes, I want to hear solutions or alternatives because what we all can agree on is that some things needed to change." I saw some head nods, blank stares, and still a few eye rolls with another audible scoff from Nancy.

Surprisingly, many people had good suggestions, but no other complaints related to any of the changes I had made. We discussed staffing, clarified job descriptions and expectations, and other plans to improve the work environment. I took meticulous notes, highlighting the things that could be easily fixed. The first meeting was counted as a success.

The evening shift was met with sandwiches and chips from Jason's Deli. I added a variety of cookies and some fresh fruit. Once again most of the group was appreciative. The night shift had more complaints and less feedback on how things could improve.

In all, the meetings were a success; all the fear and anxiety I had about dealing with certain staff members was so unnecessary, those people were harmless and backed down easily.

I decided to place a communication box outside of the offices for staff to communicate issues they may not feel comfortable talking about in front of others. After the meetings, two of the older Black staff members, Mrs. Taylor and Mrs. Smith, hung around and congratulated me on a job well done. Then hit me with some insight I had already confirmed with Daniel.

"You know, you are the first Black supervisor Lotus Gardens has ever had, and some of these old heads don't like that. They won't say it, but I've worked with them long enough to know where they stand on the race thing and being told what to do by you," Mrs. Taylor said.

"Yea, but baby just do your job and don't let them intimidate you because they will try to. You'll do good because you want to do what's best for this place." Mrs. Smith's words were encouraging.

They spoke of personal experiences they've had with other staff members that were clearly racist. The incidents were upsetting to hear, but I had to be careful not to let this conversation impact the way I moved as a supervisor because that would backfire on me. I had to be open and fair and handle each situation individually and without bias. This was going to be a challenge, especially since I already had a few stories of my own about dealing with certain non-Black staff members.

My first task was going to be a difficult one. Many staff members complained that some of the assisted living residents were requiring more help than assisted living usually provided. Nursing aids were spending extra time with these residents that may need skilled nursing services. This meant losing these paying residents in an effort to get them the care they needed and decreasing the unnecessary workload on the staff. I was nervous to have that conversation with my boss, but it was my job. Next would be asking for more funds to hire more people. The facility was beautiful and, on the surface, looked well-staffed and efficiently ran, but the truth was there was burnout, excessive overtime, and high turnover. I would be asking to relocate residents who required more assistance and to hire more people, both had a negative impact on the facility's budget. I wrote down all the information I needed to present to my boss, Mr. Bryan's son, Mark. He was also difficult to deal with.

I called Mark and let him know the concerns and surprisingly he was open to the changes. He was well aware we would lose some residents to long-term care. I found out the Bryans were part owners of an affluent nursing home nearby. I was asked to have the admission case manager contact the families and assist them in making decisions for their loved ones. As for hiring more staff, that was a harder battle that had to be re-visited later. I was thankful it was an easy but impactful win for the facility; hopefully, it would help the staff see I was serious about improvement.

CHAPTER 7

Meeting Roy

Mondays were always the day I started my "new day, new me" regimen. Consistency wasn't my strong point, but I had a solid foundation for procrastination. I had woken up early, gotten ready, went for my coffee, but opted for a large fruit cup instead of the regular croissant. For lunch I had a Caesar salad and decided to end my day with a walk in the park. I wasn't completely out of shape, but the past months of careless habits had taken a toll on my stamina.

I decided to start a light jog when I heard heavy breathing behind me. I looked over my shoulder and caught a glance of a tall nice-looking man. His stride quickened, passing me up. I maintained my slow and steady jog only to be lapped one more time by him. When I was done, he was standing by a bench stretching and staring me down. My exertion and sweat kept me from returning the stare.

The next day, I started with a walk then progressed to a jog. Just as I was starting to struggle, I was lapped by the same man from the day before. He looked more like a teenager upon further examination. We repeated the same scenario as the day before, except this time he spoke.

"What's up, lady?" He had a beautiful, dimpled smile.

"Just trying to get a workout in," I responded, trying not to sound too breathless.

"Yea, I see. You're looking good," he said.

"Ha, Ha, very funny." My sarcasm slipped out.

"Come have a seat next to me." He patted the bench.

"No, I'm sweaty and better get home."

"I ain't scared of a little sweat, come on, oblige me."

"Okay, only because I'm exhausted and probably can't make it to my car right now." I sat on the opposite side of the bench.

"I'm Roy." He held out his hand.

"Lee," I said, shaking it.

"I haven't seen you here before."

"Well, I used to come all the time but fell off. Now I'm back," I sang, trying to make light of my one of many returns to health.

"Well, that's a good thing, you got a nice little jog on you. I could give you some pointers, though."

I was beginning to think he may be a personal trainer seeking his next desperate client, which was not me. "So, you like running not jogging." I dug for information.

"Yea and working out at the gym, it's a good stress reliever."

"Stress? You look like a baby. What do you have to stress about?" I gave him a playful punch on the arm.

"What! Ms. Lady, I'm twenty-six years old. How old are you if you don't mind me asking?"

"I just turned thirty."

"That's cool." His wide smile displayed braces and was a complement to his broad nose and dimples. My eyes traveled down his arms stopping at his big hands laced with thick veins. I imagined how they would feel gripping my ass. Damn this young man was fine. "Hey, you like comedy shows?" His words brought me back to reality.

"Yea, I haven't been to one in a while."

"My boy is having a show tonight. I wasn't going, but if I get a date I will. So, you want to go with me. He's funny as hell." Roy was direct; I liked that.

"Okay, sounds like fun. I can meet you out there. Which club?"

"Great, it's Club Comedy, by the mall. Show starts at 8 p.m., let's meet up at 7:30 p.m. so I can buy you a drink."

"Okay cool, I'll be there." Wow, I hadn't been asked out in a while; I was excited.

Roy stood up and looked down at me. "Lee, please don't stand me up." I couldn't tell if he was just being serious or had control and trust issues. I erased my overthinking and answered back.

"Roy, I plan on being there, most definitely, don't worry." We said an awkward goodbye and parted ways.

Texas weather was crazy, especially in the fall. It was hot during the day and in a snap a cold front came in. It was a perfect time for me to finally wear my black thigh high boots. I squeezed into some dark skinny jeans and opted for a black off the shoulder sweater with silver jewelry to accent. My hair was pulled back in a tight ponytail and with curls brushed out for the puffy look. My deep red lipstick was offset by a simple eye with just eyeliner and mascara.

It was 7:15 p.m. and the parking lot was packed. I realized we hadn't exchange numbers, but I was hoping to find him quickly. Crowded places weren't my thing, but I was looking forward to seeing him. Luckily, his height made him stand out. He spotted me at the same time, both of us had wide grins as we walked toward each other.

"Lee, I'm so glad you came. Follow me, I got us a table in the front."

We shared a table with another couple; Roy's fraternity brother and his young gorgeous fiancé.

"Lee, meet Carlos and Cynthia. This is Lee," Roy introduced us. He called the server over and ordered a round of drinks. Carlos and Cynthia were a very affectionate couple to the point of weird for me. The show started just as I was feeling a slight buzz and was ready to laugh. The comedian was a well-built chocolate dude with short dreads, and he kept everyone laughing mostly joking about relationships and sex.

Roy took me backstage after the show and introduced me to his comedian friend. Roy knew a lot of people and they all were happy to see him with someone. We went to another spot and continued to have more drinks, eat tacos, and socialize. Roy was the life of the party and kept everyone entertained. We called it a night around 12:30 a.m. This time we did exchange numbers.

Roy was good for me. He liked to go out to restaurants, bars, movies, and clubs. My weekends were full when he was added to the equation. It was nice getting out of the house instead of waiting on Mike to come over. I loved going out with him; we were a good-looking couple who turned heads. We liked hanging together and there was no making out or sex. That was good but would be short lived.

Roy was a much-needed distraction from Mike, and I had finally given in to the flirty temptation that had been living between us. My suspicion of him being a great lover was confirmed by the numerous times he brought me to climax. It was safe to say that he had me wide open literally and figuratively. Now that the door was open, he was heavy competition for Mike. He did things Mike did not do, and his head game was a chef's kiss, superb. Roy definitely made his way to the top.

Roy knocked on the door at 1 a.m. He had given me the courtesy of calling on his way from the club. Luckily I was the one he wanted to be with tonight. The strappy, black crotchless lingerie hidden underneath a sheer robe made me a little self-conscious, but I knew what he was coming for, so the courage to even put it on was worth it.

"Hey, baby." He immediately embraced me.

"Hey, Roy," I backed up and slowly opened my robe, revealing the black leather straps tightly hugging my body.

"Oh fuck," his voice was low and rough. "Come here, baby." His dick was already hard. I dropped my robe, turned so he could get the full view, and led him to my candle-lit bedroom.

He grabbed me as soon as we hit the room, giving me a hard tongue-filled kiss. I slid on the bed and spread my legs for his viewing pleasure. Roy crawled on the bed, lifted my legs, and put them over his shoulders. He went right in and gave my pussy a long slow lick followed by several lengthy gentle kisses. Roy ate me with passion; his liquored breath warmed my pussy as his tongue softly twirled, stiffened, and glided up and down, bringing me to pure ecstasy before he indulged me with the dick. He ripped open a condom, I took it from him, slid it down his long, hard shaft and followed it with a slow lick. He lifted my head and anxiously gave me another hungry kiss. He entered me and rocked me to heaven. I slowed him down so I could take control, rolled on top of him, and repositioned my hips as Roy grabbed the straps trying to control the rhythm. He yielded to my rhythm and groaned as I rode him until we both came. I was laying on his chest when my phone dinged.

"Who the fuck is that? It's 2:30 a.m." Roy sat up.

I grabbed the phone and saw a text from Mike. **Hey Lee, just wanted you to know I miss and I'm thinking about you.** I quickly deleted it.

"It's one of those sale reminders," I uttered, too tired to tell Roy to mind his business.

"Okay, yeah right." He laid back down. "So Lee, we been messing with each other for a while, and you know I care for you. But if you got other shit going on, let me fuckin' know because I don't want to start catching feelings and shit, you know."

"Roy, we have fun together and I told you I wasn't looking for anything serious. I like you, but just want to have a little fun after coming out of a pretty bad relationship."

"I don't mean serious, but I ain't trynna be with a chick that's fuckin' around with other dudes either."

"Okay, but what about you? You fuckin' around with other women, right?" I knew what the answer was. He wanted me to be exclusive to him, but as soon as he got a chance, he would not be exclusive to me. "Don't get me wrong, I ain't out here hoein,' but you can't ask me to do something you not willing to do," I said bluntly.

"I ain't fuckin' with anyone but you now."

"Okay, for how long? Until you see someone else, right? Let's just stay like this, so no one will get their feelings hurt."

"Just stay friends…yea, right. Imma head out, Lee. I'll see you later." He got up, dressed, and left.

That conversation changed our whole vibe, the tables began to turn, but things were not going to go in my favor.

CHAPTER 8

Reality of the Holidays

Christmas was two weeks away and Roy said he had family plans and Mike had made promises of us spending time together. I was reluctantly becoming the woman I never wanted to be. The one that sat waiting for a man to do whatever bullshit it took to get away from his wife, just to come and give half himself to me. Being disgusted with the whole situation wasn't enough for me to stop playing second base. I couldn't help my heart did flips when he walked through my door, or we had so much in common it was scary. My brain would plead with my heart all the clichés. *You're so much better than this, why you let him disrespect you, just get rid of his ass,* and the all too common one, *how you get him is how you lose him.* Truth was, I may have been falling for him, but not to the extent I wanted him to leave his wife; he still was an asshole in many ways. He also made it clear leaving her was not going to happen. The phone rang while I was washing dishes.

"Hey, Lee. What you doing?" It was Johnathon.

"I'm cleaning the kitchen, getting ready for Mike to come over tonight." I instantly regretted saying that.

"Really? You actually hanging out with him this close to the holiday?" His voice oozed with sarcasm.

"Well yea, of course he would make time for me." My voice… false reassurance.

"You should really hear yourself," he continued.

"Ok, I know. Please don't start with me. I just want to have a good time. Anyway, when the new year gets going, Imma be done with him; just work on myself. Yes, I'm a fuckin' mess, I admit, but not trynna hear it right now." I tried to shut him down.

"I'm glad you can admit that. Anyway, my company Christmas party is this evening, so that's what I'm doing."

"See, you got stuff going on anyway."

"It ends at 10 p.m., the night will still be young. I wanted to chill with you afterwards, but never mind."

"We still doing our last-minute Christmas shopping tomorrow, right?" I reminded him.

"Yea. We gotta get out there early; the stores will be packed, and I still need to mail stuff off. I'm getting off this phone and wrap this secret Santa gift, I'll talk to you later." He hung up before I said bye. The mention of Mike always puts him in a shitty mood.

I shook off the bad vibes and continued getting ready. When the apartment was done, I pulled on some denim capris and a red long sleeved fitted shirt. My hair was tamed with a tight headband, and gold hoop earrings complemented my red lip gloss, gold tinted bronzer, and eyeliner.

It was 7 p.m. and still nothing from Mike, no text, no call, nothing. I just knew he didn't stand me up! I was getting more heated as the minutes ticked by. Soon 8:30, 9:00, 9:30 came and went. I stopped waiting at 10 p.m. I didn't call or text him because our plans were clear, and he knew I was waiting. By 10:30 it was official, I had been stood up. *Well Leesha, that's what your ass gets, fucking with someone that don't belong to you; stupid, just stupid.* I tried crying, but my pride wouldn't let me. There was no way I was going to sit there and look dumber than I already did. Examining my red Christmas themed nails, I thought about how to dull the sting of this disappointment. Should I call Roy? Nope, he was being an asshole, too. I can wait for Johnathon to get home and chill with him... Nope, he would just talk shit about me getting stood up or be in his feelings about being the "last resort." *I'm going to just sit my ass down here and drink some wine.*

Awakened by the unusually loud noise of Johnathon unlocking his door, I jumped up and opened mine, just as he got his door opened. Johnathon turned and peered at me as if to say, *'what the hell you want?'* He was obviously drunk, but he looked out of it and was annoyed at the sight of me.

"Hey, how was the party?" I asked, feeling awkward. He looked at me, went into his apartment, and shut the door. That added to my night of rejection. I went inside, undressed, and went to bed. The bottle of wine I had drank ushered me back to sleep.

I woke up around 10 a.m. and checked my phone, no call from Mike or Johnathon. I got ready to go shopping as planned and waited for about thirty more minutes, hoping Johnathon would call and be ready to go, as if he hadn't just shut the door on me last night. Finally, I heard some movement in his apartment and went over. He swung the door open and walked away. I noticed he wasn't dressed.

"Are we still doing last minute Christmas shopping?" I said in a false cheerful voice.

"Yea, yea right. I forgot. Let me get ready." He put his head in his hands and sat there.

"Johnathon, what's wrong with you?" He was hung over, but this was different.

"Nothing, damn..." Once again showing his annoyance.

"Ok." I sat there for a second and quickly was over it, tired of being in places and around people where I clearly wasn't wanted. "I'm gonna go." I got up and headed toward the door.

"No, just wait," he called out.

"No, clearly, I'm not wanted here, so I'm good. Bye."

"Just fuckin' wait! It was an eventful night, and I did the stupidest shit ever."

"What?" Curiosity stopped me in my tracks.

"You know I went to the company Christmas party, right? Well, me and a couple of coworkers got sloppy... I mean sloppy drunk."

"Really, Johnathon? No playing it cool with coworkers, I guess."

"Right… well we ended up and Zia's place, she lives like five minutes away from the office. So, me, Zia, and Rosalyn… well we were drinking and shit." His head hung low.

"Okay, got it, you all were drunk," I said, encouraging him to get to the point.

"We start fucking around, and Zia asked about the rumors about me, and I told them, yes, I was bi, and they couldn't believe it. Rosalyn was like *'you need to fuck with a bitch like me,'* then Zia was like *'no, I'm the type of bitch you need.'* So, they both was throwin' pussy at that point. They both was sucking dick and everything, I just let the shit happen and had a fuckin' threesome. I can't believe I did some shit like that with coworkers! How stupid is that?" He clearly was ashamed and disappointed about ruining his overly professional reputation.

"Really, Johnathon! You slipped and fell in not one, but two vaginas?" I was a little hurt, but had to remember he was not my man, and I was just pacing the floors for a man who stood me up.

"I really did accidently slip and fall, I was so fucking drunk," he confessed. "On the cool though, I think they be fuckin' with each other anyway because they were moving as if they knew what each other liked, too." His lips curled into a small smirk.

"Oh, you literally was just the fuck boy." I couldn't hold back my laugh.

"Literally, I was just the fuck boy." He shook his head in fake disgust then we both busted out laughing.

"You walk around here with an attitude, like you were forced into some pussy!" We were cracking up by now.

"I was! I didn't want no work pussy! That Jack Daniels wanted that shit."

"Well, since you were assaulted last night, do you still wanna go shopping?"

"Oh, now you a comedian with bad jokes? Yes, I need some shopping therapy; let me get dressed." He disappeared into his bedroom.

CHAPTER 9

Holiday Rain

Johnathon and I spent a lot of time over celebrating the holidays together. Johnathon couldn't drag me everywhere he went, so I was forced to spend some time alone. In my typical ill-advised style, I decided to go to a club up the street for a few drinks. After squeezing into a little black dress, stiletto heels, and adding a pair of big rhinestone earrings to complement my big hair, I ventured out looking for a good time.

I sat at the bar and ordered the only drink I intended on buying myself after seeing a few guys eyeing me. As I suspected, my next two drinks were compliments of whomever. I did entertain some conversations, but my disinterest was apparent because none hung around for any length of time.

Then someone gave my shoulder a squeeze and followed it with a backrub. I quickly turned around to see who had the audacity to come up and start touching me like that. There stood Darnell, his stunning midnight skin offset by a creamy button-down. Oh shit! Darnell, standing here, was proof that the devil was busy. His presence was the cherry on top of a shit-filled cake. Our eyes locked in anger… or was it passion?

"Well, isn't it the devil himself, please don't touch me." I decided anger was the safest option. Darnell held both hands up as if he were surrendering to the police.

"Yes ma'am. I just wanted to say hi to you, it's been a long time. I didn't mean any harm, Ms. Leesha." His irritating grin sent a tingle through my stomach.

"You harm me, ha… not possible." I motioned to the bartender for another drink.

"Oh, I know I ain't got shit on you, but that don't change the fact that I miss you." He leaned in closer, breath heating my ear. "Miss all of you, miss that soft, wet pussy, too." His hand was once again on my back. I pulled away.

"Wow, let's get right to the point shall we. Get away from me, Darnell." My voice was not convincing as I squirmed on the stool now. Uncomfortable couldn't even begin to describe the feeling he stirred in me.

"You ain't got to use that stool to massage that pussy, you know. We have our differences, but one thing we have in common is the fact that my dick fits perfectly in that tight ass pussy. Why don't you let me get at it one last time? No fucking strings. I won't be harassing you or anything. I promise I can control myself." His hand had migrated up to my neck, joining his lips as he gently kissed me.

"You got your fucking nerves; like I said, get away from me." I was still standing strong.

"You mean to tell me, your fuckin' body ain't calling for me right now. Are you gonna deny yourself this Christmas present? It's late, we both alone. Come on, I just wanna make you feel good; who the fuck gonna know?" The tequila shot I drank made him sound unusually rational.

"I will know, you conceited bastard, and that matters more than anyone." I was appalled at the audacity, but intrigued by the offer.

"Okay, tell me 'No' then." Darnell backed away, daring me to send his ass packing.

The alcohol and overwhelming loneliness refused to say that simple word. *No, come on Leesha, tell his ass no!* I just looked at him. He held out his hand and I grabbed it as he led me to the devil's playground, the place I knew would be filled with regret. Hopefully, the orgasm would be worth it.

Why I insisted on my place was beyond reason. I told myself it would be easier if I were already home, so I could just pass out afterward. Not thinking about the fact, I didn't want Darnell to know where I lived in the first place. But there I was at my home, adding to the many bad spirits that had already crossed my threshold.

Darnell went to work as soon as we got in my bedroom. *Please let this be worth it.* He kissed me as if I were a craving he was finally satisfying, and I was happy to quench his thirst. He peeled off my dress as I kicked my heels off. His thick fingers slipped through the side of my panties and began to aggressively massage my pussy. *Oh God, Oh God!* Finally, he slipped them inside as I dropped to my bed, even more relaxed by the texture of my soft pink comforter. He worked the inside of my pussy, rubbing my walls until I started raining. His body slid down mine, making me breathless with anticipation, heart beating out of my chest. He inhaled deeply, smelling my pussy with his head lingering between my legs.

"God Damn! I miss this fucking pussy." He took a long lick and started sucking my clit, making me squeal. "Fuck, aw fuck you taste like that shit you been drinking, so fucking good baby, Imma get drunk off this shit." Then came the thunderstorm originating from my stomach and sprinkling his tongue. "That's right, baby," he coached my pussy as I came. Darnell was the fucking rainmaker. Finally, he came up, grabbed my hips, and slid his dick in with just the right amount of force.

"Oh, yes, yes..." I panted, moving my hips frantically, desperate for the next downpour.

"You want this dick, baby girl... show me, yea, that's right, keep fucking me back." Darnell's strong stroke turned into the perfect pounding that I knew was coming. That rhythmic, hard pressure drove me crazy. His dick game always backed up that dirty mouth and never disappointed.

"Oh God, Oh God, yes." I clasped my hands over my mouth to muffle my screams as my waters flooded the rainmaker's dick.

"That's right, get yours, baby, cum on that dick." His pace quickened as he finally came with a loud groan, his body collapsed on mine.

Damn, Darnell did it again and I was not disappointed and had absolutely no regrets. He immediately fell asleep, giving me the impression my job was done, too. I grabbed my sore left ear and yanked my earring off and automatically went for the right one, which was missing. I searched for it around my pillows and looked over the edge of the bed but couldn't find it. Shit, I had just brought those and already lost one. I would continue the search in the morning; Right now, I want to enjoy my still tingling body.

I woke up to Darnell getting dressed. Oh yes… there was the ever-fleeting regret coming over me. Disappointed in my lapse of judgement, I projected my anger at him.

"Got what you wanted, now you leaving? No goodbye, no fuck you, no nothing? You just walking out the door, right? You got what you wanted, so you up and gone?" I tried to keep my voice nonchalant and steady.

"If I'm not mistaken, you got what you wanted too, three or four times if I counted correctly," he shot back.

"Just three, so don't flatter yourself too much."

"Three is good, last I checked." He crotched down by my bed, his face close to mine.

"Lee, you already know, you my heart, but we fight like cats and dogs. Sex, that shit is bomb, though. Remember, I said no strings and you agreed. Call me anytime you need me, I'll be happy to oblige." He gave me as slow teasing kiss. "Three times is a guarantee." He slipped his shirt on and walked out. I hated him and was pissed at myself, too, but the effects of the tequila took me back to an unsettled sleep.

I got up about noon, took a shower, opened my patio door letting the chilly air in, and started doing laundry. I wanted to get the smell of Darnell out of my home, off of me. I stripped my bed, put on some new sheets, and vacuumed my floor. There was a Magnum condom wrapper strategically placed on my dresser by the door, on display for anyone walking in. I threw it away covering it with the other trash. My stomach dropped when I heard the knock on my door. I knew who it was.

"Hey Johnathon, what's up? Come in." I was extra cheerful, but he didn't respond. He slowly held up a shiny object. I took a closer look and realized it was my missing earring. "Oh, my earring! Where did you find it?" I grabbed it, noticing it was all bent up. "What happened to it?"

"Your man stepped on the shit walking out the door this morning. He just looked down and kicked it aside with no regard." The disgusted look on his face let me know this conversation wasn't going to be pleasant. "Oh, Leesha's blank stare is all I get." His jaw tightened.

"I'm just wondering where all this anger is coming from, friend." That was the absolute wrong thing to say, but now I was on the defense.

Johnathon snatched the earring back and threw it against the wall. "That asshole looked me dead in the face and said if I was coming to see you, for sure, you were too tired for anyone else. He didn't even care to pick your shit up and hold it for you. I hate to see a nigga like that treating you like shit; and you too damn blind to see, too stupid to care, or too fucking desperate to acknowledge it."

Johnathon's face was so close to mine I could feel his body heat. Tears stung my eyes as I stumbled back and flopped on the couch. I covered my face and stopped breathing to keep from crying. My efforts were futile, and I burst into tears. Pain pierced my chest, and I couldn't tell if my heart stopped or if it was racing. Sliding to the floor, solely depending on my knees to hold me up… Johnathon kneeled next to me. He hugged me as I sobbed and clinched my chest, certain I was having a heart attack. He grabbed my hand and placed it on his chest.

"Breathe, just breathe. Mirror my breaths. Feel my heart, close your eyes." Johnathon was talking me out of this endless anxiety attack. "I'm here for you, Lee, always will be. Do you hear me? Always, no matter what." He knew I needed to hear that because not only did I feel bad for sleeping with Darnell, but my greatest fear was losing

Johnathon or his respect. Truth was, at this point I didn't even respect myself.

"But you're mad at me, and I can't take that shit Johnathon; I can't. I'm sorry, he was an old boyfriend, we were together for almost a year. I was sad, lonely, I don't know... why, why, I do stupid shit like that. I don't ever expect anyone to love me or even really want me. But I do know one thing, at least I'm desired. If that is the only intimacy I can get, then I guess that's what I'll take. I'm not proud of it, but it is the truth. Even you can't think of me past the friendship status, but sex, yea you'll do that, real love, a real relationship with me... no." I was as honest with him as he had just been with me. Johnathon was silent, carefully thinking of what to say next.

"Leesha, it's not that I don't love you or can't even think of being in a relationship with you; matter of fact, it's quite the opposite. But you make me crazy, angry, sad, whatever emotion I can't fucking deal with you bring it out. I would seriously consider being with you, but I couldn't trust you and frankly you couldn't and shouldn't trust me because we are looking for someone to love us through our mess. The shit that only can come from within. We too fucking broken to go there with each other. I'd rather have an unconditional friendship that would last forever with you than a crazy love affair that will break us. Yea, I slipped up with you and I know that plays with your emotions. It plays with mine, too. Just know that like this, I am here for you always, and will never leave you, never." His words calmed me, but they still hurt.

My chest pain slowly subsided, but my feelings were still raw. In an effort to combat my loneliness, to take up space in my head, and forget about Mike and Roy, I went backwards, with Darnell of all people. How low could I go for a few moments of pleasure? Now here I was looking like a damn hoe bag to Johnathon. How could I win, be a better person, not be so desperate for whatever? Truth was that all these men wanted sex and I was acting like that was all I had to offer. I tricked myself into behaving like they expected me to. I sat staring out the patio door, and of course, it started raining.

CHAPTER 10

Post Holiday Contact

Christmas and New Years went by and nothing from Mike or Roy, and Darnell wasn't even a thought. My plan to visit my mother in Louisiana was derailed when her husband, James, had a heart attack. I still wanted to go support them, but Mom said she rather I stayed home so she could focus on being with James at the hospital. James wanted me to come because Mom would be forced to take a break from him, but she refused to leave his side and promised I could see them when he recovered.

Johnathon and I spent the holidays house hopping between friends and coworkers. We stayed tipsy and high the whole time. Nurses were calling out of work like crazy, so I had to cover some shifts at the facility, which made me regret partying so hard with Johnathon. For the new year I had to calm it down with him. We loved hanging out and partying together, but I stayed foggy and hungover. It was a way to numb my wounded ego and forget about the rejection. That type of fun was taking a toll on my mind and my body. I had gained at least eleven pounds from Thanksgiving to New Years.

Truth be told, my whole damn life was messed up from what I thought was fun at one time. Men, sex, alcohol, and everything else I was doing was like being on a hamster wheel, running nowhere fast. I realized I had no personal goals or plans, living day by day waiting for the next booty call or whatever. Why did I settle for this shit? Why did I do anything to not be alone and chose to deal with men that cannot commit to me. But the universe was on my side and forcing Mike and Roy out of my life. There was still no word from them, and I decided not to answer if they called.

The holidays were over, and work was finally calming down, people stopped calling in and Daniel was back from his annual month-long vacation. I had taken the day off to wind down, lay around, and watch movies. There was a light knock at my door, which I really wanted to ignore. The next knock was slightly louder. I put on my robe and looked out the peephole, only to see Mike standing there. I went back to my bedroom and wrapped myself tightly in my comforter. *Fuck him*, I thought as I pushed play to continue my movie. I didn't want to be bothered. After a couple more knocks, he left, and I was glad.

A few hours later, Roy's name flashed across the phone. I pressed decline and threw my phone across the bed. Now they had time; the important times are over and time to call me. Nope, not today.

Falling asleep with a lot on my mind and a little alcohol in my system wasn't a good idea. Nightmares dragged me through an unstable sleep-wake cycle. My dad's voice screamed insults and other words my young mind did not understand. The closet I ran into to get away was now utilized as my prison for simply existing, was filled with demons screaming in my face, but always stopping short of a physical attack.

"You ruin everything, just like your mom did! Worthless! You're fucking worthless." His voice was not human. To me, it was the devil growling every word and threatening my life. Verbal abuse coupled with the demons enclosed in that small space was an eternal fall to hell. I cried and screamed, my terror angering the devil on the other side of the door.

The fight with my sheets woke me up. I jumped from the bed and ran to the bathroom, barely making it to the toilet before I started peeing. My mind was still confused, and I cried as the sensation of releasing my nervous bladder overcame me. Looking around, I realized I was not in that dark closet, and was not the little girl who would urinate on the floor when fear strangled all senses and control. I had grown up, in my own safe place, and the devil was dead.

Still exhausted from the night before, I laid in bed a little longer than planned. Later, I decided to go wash my car and get some groceries for the week. My heart raced when I saw Mike in a dark grey suit accented with a maroon tie and shoes, sitting on my car. He jumped up when he saw me, and I just walked around him to open the door to get in. He reached over and slammed it, blocking my way. The aroma of his masculine, sweet cologne pierced my nostrils, angering me more. Why was Mike's presence so intoxicating. Part of me wanted to hear him out, the other part wanted him as far away as possible.

"I'm sorry, Lee…I know you're mad, but I had no choice."

"Get the fuck out my way. Who cares about your choices? Apparently, I wasn't a choice. You didn't choose to spend any time with me, so it looks like we're done here." I tried to get to my door and was blocked once again. "Mike, don't make me slap the shit out of you."

"Go ahead, I deserve it…I fucked up. Trish's family came in town and…"

"I couldn't give two fucks about Trish's family being in town. But you're married, you were right where you were supposed to be, but you are not supposed to be here. Now move!" I yelled.

Mike threw his hands up and stepped aside. I got in my car and took off without even looking at him. The car wash was three blocks down. I pulled in and sat there, heart pounding and tears stinging my eyes. All I could do was hit the stirring wheel, angry at him for treating me this way, angry at myself for being in this position. Really, he was supposed to be with her for God's sake! She was his wife!

Why? Why do I care about this mess? Why do I care about him? But did I really care about that man? I was humiliated about the fact I was fucking two men who didn't give two shits about even seeing me around the holidays. Whatever, all of this was my fault. I got out, walked around my very dirty black Nissan Maxima, and quickly got back in because the tears wouldn't stop falling. With all my energy drained, I decided against washing the car and would just get the necessities at the grocery store.

Johnathon was working and his comments about Mike were unnecessary right now. So, I called Mikayla to have lunch and we met at our favorite all you can eat sushi spot.

"Hey, girl, I'm glad you called, I was sitting around bored. What's going on with you?" Mikayla was her regular cheerful self.

"I'm good. Me and Johnathon really enjoyed your family's Christmas party, thanks for inviting us."

"You both are always welcome. Johnathon was definitely the life of the party, and don't think I didn't notice you and my cousin flirting all night. He's been asking about you."

"Really? He was cool, tell him I said hi." I was nonchalant because I didn't want Mikayla to know I had a quick make out session with her cousin in his car when we went on the ice run. A one-night stand followed two days later, then I ghosted him. I admit my behavior the past months was filled with not so proud moments.

"Okay, I'll tell him. Didn't you two exchange numbers? I thought you would have gotten together by now."

"Um yea, he's nice, maybe we will get together, but now is not the right time."

"Right... now is not the time because you're too busy entertaining Mr. Married Man and Young Boy Roy." She rolled her eyes.

"No, that's not it. I just want to be left alone, that's all. Anyway, tell me about the job and this new man you're dating." It was time for a subject change. Mikayla was all too happy to update me on her work and love life. The next two hours were filled with Mikayla's nonstop talking about her perfect life. But I didn't mind, her happiness made me happy. It was an escape from my bullshit and gave a glimpse of what life was supposed to be when good decisions were made with optimism and hope instead of careless decisions rendered out of toxicity, trauma, and disappointments.

Roy called that evening. I swear he was on the same wavelength as Mike. Whenever Mike popped up, he was never far behind. But Roy didn't make promises he didn't intend on keeping, so I halfway knew I wasn't going to hear from him. He spent the holidays with family and his cousin who was home from a deployment. But I still didn't answer his call because there was no reason to. Truth be told, a part of me knew it was past time to let go, but…. I didn't even know what my "but" was. I didn't know why I latched to these relationships that served no purpose but to reduce me to a person that I don't even like or respect; my actions, decisions, and quite frankly my thought process was all fucked up. Would I do anything about it? More validation I needed to find a good therapist.

CHAPTER 11

Weakness Wins

Mike did not give up. He was at the coffee shop every morning and tapped at my door every other evening for two weeks straight. I gave no words or acknowledgement to him. Why should I? I was just the side chick who was done.

It was late Thursday afternoon when I pulled up to my apartment building. I was grabbing bags out the car when I heard Mike calling my name. I turned around and there he was, holding a small red shiny box, wrapped in gold ribbon.

"You can't be serious, now you want to come with a Christmas gift? Really, get the fuck out my face." I was insulted.

"Lee, this has been in my glove box since before Christmas. Just let me talk to you for a moment," he pleaded.

"A moment has passed, get out of my way." I didn't want to give him a chance to get near me.

"No, all I want to do is apologize and get back to where we used to be. Okay, I fucked up, but you know how things are, and you know I fuckin' need you... I need you, Lee." Mike's face was close to mine. His body was so close. His energy was making me weak. My mind warned me not to look into his eyes, but I did and instantly felt the wall I had built for a month begin to crack. "Please, I miss you so much. Just talk to me."

"I don't feel like there is much to say. Mike, you are married, and I hate being in this position. I hate caring that you forgot me on Christmas. I hate accepting the fact that I am messing with someone that will never put me first. My time is precious, and my life should be more than just sitting around waiting on you."

"Do you think I like being in this situation? I never fuckin' thought I would fall for you, but this shit is making me crazy. I need to be with you. No, I don't want you sitting around waiting on me, but you ain't just twiddling your thumbs… Leesha, I know you seeing someone else and probably fuckin' that dude next door to you, with his nosey ass." He was trying that reverse psychology shit, like I was just as bad as he was. Was I?

"You got some mutha fuckin' audacity, speculating about who I let in my bed, when you lay with someone every night!"

"I know, I shouldn't have gone there, but you are acting like I'm the damn devil and just running around here trying to break your heart. Please, just please forgive me." He stood back with one hand in his pocket and the other balled in a fist almost crushing the small red box.

"Give me the damn box." I snatched it and began walking away. He stood there and watched until I walked into the building, then he got into his car and drove away.

I dropped the bags and opened the box as soon as I made it through my door. The sparkly diamond earrings were beautiful but didn't erase my disappointment. I was hoping to stay strong. Then, right on cue my phone chimed with a message. It was Roy asking to come over. I waited ten minutes then responded, **Yes, come over.** What better way to get Mike off my mind than to entertain Roy?

Roy and I sat on the couch eating popcorn and acting like we were into the movie, both ignoring the constant ding of his phone alerting of messages. He looked uneasy and finally turned his phone off. Obviously, he had something going on.

We got more comfortable as the evening went on. The truth was we were waiting for the other to make a move. He looked so good I was aching for him. He finally made his way to my side of the couch and started rubbing my leg.

"I missed you and that sexy ass body." He kissed my neck.

"Oh really, I couldn't tell, but I hope your holidays were good."

"They were okay. I played uncle. My sister and her husband needed some time away from the kids. My cousin was too busy chasing ass to hang out with me. I was good with the kids if I say so myself." He turned my head toward him and kissed me. I missed his sensual, out of control lips.

The desperation we felt was evident in our hungry kiss as we quickly removed each other's clothes. I straddled him, slid him into me, exhaled in relief, and began to slowly ride. Gliding up and down and using my thick hips to draw circles on his dick made him groan and squeeze my waist in an effort to regain his control. He grabbed my breast whispering "fuck" as he slid it into his mouth kissing and softly biting it. Right before he was going to lose control, he lifted me off him, hastily laying me on the couch and dropping his head between my legs, then devouring my pussy. I moaned as he came back up and slid into me. I braced myself for an explosive finish and gripped the arm of the couch. He quickly brought me to ecstasy and squeezed me tight as he came.

"Damn, I missed you," Roy panted.

"I missed you, too. Wow, I think you trying to turn me out," I said.

"Naw, just trying to keep you for myself." His eyes tried to capture mine. I avoided them.

"You hear me, Lee? I want to be done with this *just friends* shit."

"Why are you going there, Roy. I think being friends is okay for us."

"Yea, but we are fucking, I don't fuck friends." His clinched jaw and wrinkled forehead were signs this conversation needed to end.

"Obviously you do and it's also obvious someone is looking for you right now, and it ain't no friend. Why do we have the same conversation, knowing you got other shit going on, too," I continued challenging him.

"Okay, just fuck it then. I got to go, see you later, *friend.*" He reached out his hand for me to shake it.

"Really, Roy, we're shaking hands now?" I knew he wasn't happy, and I would pay for this later.

"Yeah, bruh, see you later." He finished fastening his belt and walked out, slamming the door.

Damn it. Why did Roy want something more with me? Why didn't I want the same was the real question. Deep down I knew the answer was because I still wanted to deal with Mike, even though everything in me warned against that, too.

Mike waited another week before he contacted me again, just long enough for me to cool down. I had seen him getting coffee and his approach was to go back to friend mode.

"Hey, Leesha. How is the job going?" he asked.

"It's going as expected." I took my coffee from Kim as I tried to keep it short.

"I hope that means things are getting better," he continued.

"They are." I continued walking.

"What are you doing for lunch? Want to meet up?" he asked.

I paused and thought for a moment, then decided to call his bluff. There was no way he was going to follow through with a public lunch with me. "Sure, did you have somewhere in mind?"

"I feel like eating Bayseas. What about you?" he asked. Bayseas was a small seafood restaurant chain, only about five in San Antonio. The food was delicious and the portions were hefty.

I loved some fried fish and shrimp, so I was down with going there. "Sure, I'll meet you there around noon?" I suggested.

"Sounds good." He smiled.

I arrived to Bayseas at noon and joined Mike at a table in the corner of the restaurant.

"Thank you for coming." His smile made me tingle. I cursed myself for feeling that way.

"I'm not turning down a good lunch, so thank you," I said, picking up the menu. I already knew I was getting the catfish and shrimp special, a loaded baked potato, and a side salad with ranch.

"You're welcome," he said as the waitress approached our table. We ordered the same except he opted for fries instead of the baked potato.

Mike started in with apologizing again. I pretended not to care anymore. He chose his words carefully and made sure he didn't mention Trisha or her family. He laid full blame on himself and his shitty time management. He lied saying he would make me a priority, which made me feel disgusted with him as a person in general. He was saying what he thought I wanted to hear. I didn't even know what I wanted to hear, there was really nothing he could say to make me feel right about this whole situationship. I enjoyed my meal and let him finish his prepared statement.

"You're barely saying anything." He rubbed his head and clasped his hands in front of his face.

"What do you think I should say? I obviously have no business even dealing with you."

"Quit saying shit like that. Yea, this ain't ideal, but I like being with you and don't want to lose you."

"Lose me? I think it's safe to say you never had me." I maintained a defiant attitude. Mike tightened his fist and lightly hit the table.

"I never lied or was secretive about my situation… my marriage." There was the Mike I knew, getting bold with his words, starting to reveal his narcissistic side. "I never once said I was looking to leave my wife, I never once thought you would get me in this fuckin' chokehold either. But it remains, that I am married, I own that shit, but you got fuckin' choices too, Lee. You can be done anytime." He challenged my weakness for him. My stomach tightened and undigested food crawled back into my throat. I took a sip of water, thinking how to respond.

"Oh, but can I be done when I want? Last I checked your ass was constantly glued to my car, knocking at my door, or ringing my phone." I threw my napkin on the table and started to get up. He grabbed my wrist and the look on my face made him release it just as quick.

"I'm sorry. I didn't come to fight with you. I came to let you know, I didn't mean to put you in this mess, but I can't control my feelings for you, and no, I don't want to lose you, not like this, not just yet."

"Oh, sure… you wanna keep fucking. You wanna have your cake and eat it, too. You want to be the only one bene-fiting… right?" My body trembled and I wanted to scream.

"No, no… I mean, yeah. Sex with you is amazing, but you are also someone I need to talk to, take some of this fuckin' stress away, have a good time with. You didn't like any of the time we spent together?" His voice softened. "Come on, Lee, you acting like you been fuckin' with me and only me. We both got our own shit. You ain't that damn wrapped up in this. Just forgive me so we can move on, please." Mike was now deflecting blame and begging at the same time. He was a piece of work.

"Mike, I can't with you. I gotta go. Thanks for lunch." I got up and walked out, regretting I agreed to come, but not surprised I felt worse.

I replayed my conversation with Mike over and over. I had such a weak spot for his no-good ass. Praying for strength to rid myself of him wasn't working. I was relying on willpower and the memory of all the annoying shit he said to keep me away from him.

I busied myself with social media when a message popped up. It was Mike. **Open the door.** My throat tightened and heart pounded as I sat frozen for a second, contemplating my next move. Against my better judgement, I opened the door and he was getting off the elevator. The stressed look on his face softened when he saw me there, obediently waiting. *Damn it, weakness prevails again.* As soon as he got to me, he leaned in and his lips captured mine. I walked backward letting him into my home, back into my life.

In a matter of minutes he was in my bed, sucking my breasts as he slowly slid his fingers in and out of me, teasing my g-spot until a steady stream of wetness coated his hand. Just the weight of his body on mine made me want to cum before he even entered me. Oh God, I missed that man. His body was the perfect mold to mine, and when he entered me, it was like cold waves crashing on hot rocks; my aching for him, finally satisfied. His strokes were slow, and I could tell he was fighting his imminent release. But me, I didn't hold back; I continued to cum two more times before his pace quickened and he surrendered to my contracting walls. I had fallen under his spell again.

Not long after, we had another falling out when his wife called while we were together. I couldn't stand listening to that conversation and acted stupid. That was another blow to my ego.

"You are getting on my nerves, Leesha! For real!" I had made the mistake of telling Mikayla about what happened with Mike. "You chose to be the fucking side piece, the mistress, the 'never number one bitch.' Now you got the nerve to be mad because he spoke to his wife in your presence. Not to mention the way he spoke to her. Can you imagine that shit? He called her an insecure psycho when she was completely sane and right about him. He is a narcissistic bastard. I can't stand his ass, and I almost can't stand you! Honestly, you should be glad you're not her, instead you're jealous. I just stay confused with you." She took a big bite of her chocolate cake and looked out the window of our favorite restaurant in the Pearl, shaking her head in frustration.

"I know..." Mikayla was right. "I'm getting on my own nerves, and I stopped being able to *stand myself* a long time ago." I was fighting tears because the truth hurt, but Mikayla was the type to deliver the truth, painful or not.

She slid next to me in the booth and dragged me into a forced hug. "Lee, I don't mean to hurt your feelings, but I wouldn't be a friend if I didn't tell you what it is."

"I know, Kay, that's why you're my girl," I admitted.

"I love you, sis." She squeezed me tighter.

"Love you, too. It takes a true friend to accept all the hoe-ish things I do." I giggled. Mikayla looked at me trying to restrain her laugh.

"You're not a hoe, girl, you just living life a little too loud and getting your feelings hurt. When you find what you're looking for, it will be better."

I took the last bite of my carrot cake and opted not to tell her about Roy, not ready to endure the words she would have for me… and dared not to mention her cousin. More confirmation I was a fucking mess.

CHAPTER 12

Ms. Franklin

The night with Johnathon and my desire to stay away from Mike and Roy reinforced the need to find someone to talk to. I Googled a therapist to which I could relate. My goal was to find a Black female, of course older than me but not too old to where I would feel judged. I decided on Ms. Cornelia Franklin.

"Hi, Leesha, it's nice to meet you."

"Hello, Ms. Franklin, nice to meet you as well."

"Tell me about yourself and what you wish to accomplish in our time together."

"Well, I recently got a new job as a supervisor in an assistant living facility, which I thought was going to be easier than my last job, but it is very challenging for me. The staff is jaded from the last supervisor. He didn't establish a good relationship with them or address any of their concerns. So now I'm here trying to pick up the pieces and not be a pushover at the same time. As a Black woman, I have to be very careful of how I deal with people, always trying not to be labeled as the "angry" or "bitchy" Black woman. So, I'm finding it hard to make the changes that need to be made, win the trust of the staff, and not let it overwhelm me." I felt the familiar tightness in my chest. Anxiety was already taking hold.

"Got it. That could be difficult to walk into a position like that, especially as a Black woman. But remember you were selected for a reason, and you will figure it out in time. Things may not be perfect but what is? We can get more into that later. So, what are you doing to manage that stress?"

"I really don't do anything for stress. Everything I do to relax, is probably not a good stress reliever," I admitted.

"Give me some examples of how you relax."

"Okay, no need to beat around the bush; drinking, overeating, sex, and... this is confidential, right?"

Ms. Franklin nodded her head yes. "Unless there is something reportable such as abuse, crimes, something dangerous to yourself or others. I'm sorry, should have started with that," she reassured me.

"Well, I do smoke, but only with my neighbor, we hang out a lot."

"Smoke marijuana?"

"A little..." I was back paddling now.

"Ok, go ahead..." She must have sensed me shutting down.

"That's it, all my bad habits."

"You said sex, so you're dating?" Ms. Franklin jumped right in.

"I'm single, just dating around. Other than that, there's not much to me."

"How many men are you dating?"

"There are two guys that I see regularly, nothing serious. To be completely honest... because I am here for help, right?" I was almost embarrassed to say. "I'm seeing a married man... and also another guy. I'm not looking for commitment, just having a little fun." I was hoping my smile would cover the unexpected tears that began stinging my eyes.

"What is making you sad about that situation?"

"I don't know... I like being with them, but after umm sex... I don't know."

"Go on," she encouraged me.

"Yea, like I said, I'm having fun. I just got out of a bad relationship, and I choose to be single and only date for now."

"Understood. You were saying, after sex, what? How do you feel?"

"Umm, sometimes I feel like that's all they want. Well, Roy, the younger one, takes me out at least, but Michael, he doesn't because we kind of lay low. But I like to think I'm the one using them to get what I want."

"Possible yes; you are using each other."

"Yea, I guess. I mean with Mike, the married one.... is using me for sex I guess, nothing more. Maybe my company because we have good conversation." I realized how ridiculous that sounded. I was forced to think about what I was using him for because actually he offered me nothing I couldn't get from anyone else, minus the wife. Feeling the need to rationalize this shit to Ms. Franklin, the foolish words continued spilling from my mouth. "Well, at least I have nothing to lose, Mike has a whole damn wife."

Ms. Franklin stared at me, twirling her pen. "Well, if you have nothing to lose, what is it you have to the gain?"

"In the long run, nothing." *Why don't you just make me feel shitty on my first visit, Ms. Franklin?* "Yea, I know I need to leave him alone, but it's hard." Finally, I decided to get real.

"We can definitely get into the weeds when it comes to your relationships, but for our next meeting, I want you to think about what your goals are personally and professionally, and what you hope to gain from our sessions."

"Insight, what I want is, some insight," I answered without even thinking.

"Insight on what?"

"On why I make decisions that always make me feel drained and terrible. Why everyone else's feelings are more important than my own." The designs on her rug shifted as the tears filled my eyes.

"What makes you say that everyone's feelings are more important than yours?" she inquired.

"Aside from the two men I told you about, I slept with my best friend." I decided to throw the rest of my cards on the table.

"Your best friend? Okay, go on." Her posture straightened, ready to hear the drama.

"Yes, he had a bad day at work, and me being old faithful, did not stop it. I just wanted him to feel better, regardless of how I knew I would feel afterward. Don't get me wrong, I was curious about sex with him because we get along so well, and he is amazingly fine. But I also knew that would be a disaster for me."

"How did you think you would feel?"

"I knew that Johnathon would never want anything with me because we know each other too well. But I didn't want him to be upset or put off with me because I denied him when he was already having a terrible day."

"But he's your friend. Do you think he would have been upset with you?"

"No, I suppose not, but I didn't want to chance it, I guess."

"Chance rejection?" She twirled her pen again and jotted more notes.

"No... I mean he would never reject me." The clarity of the conversation was confusing me. But Johnathon did reject me the next morning. I can't even say he fucked me because I've been fucked before, and it wasn't that, it felt like so much more. Then the next morning it was like 'sike, just kidding, friend.' It didn't surprise me, but there was almost a glimmer of something more; a glimmer he quickly extinguished.

Ms. Franklin paused, waiting for my words to make sense to me. Saying my thoughts aloud and hearing them made me realize how misleading my mind was versus what was really going on. That was scary, and I realized I couldn't even trust myself.

"Leesha, you know what I found most interesting about you? Where you're from, how you grew up, and your family you made no mention of." Her voice was soft but strong enough to break through my hazy thoughts. I nodded my now aching head, knowing that story was for another day.

After the awkward silence, Ms. Franklin's voice broke through again. "Our time is up, Leesha. Your homework is to think about your goals for our time together."

"Okay, I will. Thank you very much." I walked away with doubts Ms. Franklin was the right fit. Counseling was foreign to me, and that one session made my body hurt with anxiety and sadness. I wasn't ready for this.

Johnathon had been a little stand-offish, but I wanted to hang out, so I paid him a visit

"Oh hey, come in." He smiled.

"What are you doing?" I asked.

"Just chillin' right now."

"I just wanted to check on you and see how you are doing. I miss my friend." I got right to the point.

"I miss you, too. I thought I heard that dude Mike over there the other day. Sounded a little heated." He looked at me, but I couldn't tell if he was disgusted or really didn't care. It was a forced blank stare.

"Yea, long story but nothing important." I avoided that conversation. "I started counseling.

"Yea you mentioned it. How is that going?"

"I'm not sure, I know what I need to do, but doing it is different. I stay disappointing myself," I admitted.

"Sometimes we are our own worst enemies. I know how it feels to continually make fucked up decisions." He was surprisingly understanding.

"That's life, I guess." I backed away from the conversation I had originally intended.

"Hey, I'm meeting a friend for dinner tonight and I have a few errands to run before I go out. So, I'll get at you later," he abruptly said.

"Oh, okay." My feet were stuck and I couldn't move. I wanted to know who he was going out with. He was always so secretive, and I was almost an open book.

"See you later, Lee." He snapped me out of my jealous thoughts.

"Oh, yes. Okay, bye." I hurried out the door.

CHAPTER 13

Dealing with Demons

As time passed, it was obvious I still didn't want to be alone and the balancing act of separating my time between Mike and Roy became a challenge. Every time I was with one, the other was calling or texting, vying for my attention and affection. The selfish, reckless part of me didn't care whose feelings I was hurting in the process even if it was my own. I was clearly addicted to the thrill of having them both craving my time. The need to keep both in my life started to consume me, but deep down I knew this unmanageable situation was unhealthy and taking a toll. At this point, I really did care for them and the thought of losing either one made me physically sick. I knew there was no future with Mike or Roy, but these harmless relationships had taken an unexpected turn. The internal struggle between my selfish desires and my sensible side forced me to make a choice. Actually, the choice wasn't between Mike or Roy, the choice was between them or me. I wanted to choose me… for once. I was choosing myself.

And then there was Johnathon, who clearly stated we should remain just that … friends, regardless of the line we had already crossed. Our easygoing open rapport we once shared was awkward with an undercurrent of alcohol fueled sexual tension simmering between us. Johnathon would acknowledge the slow burning connection and quickly extinguish it, making me feel unsettled and frustrated. I wanted to pull back from him to avoid confusion and the temptation that lingered between us. But Johnathon remained a consistent and reliable friend, which was comforting to me. This whole situation was becoming extremely overwhelming. I was trapped in toxic chaos.

It took a while but I realized my plan to be single and have my men friends with no strings attached backfired. The purpose was to be selfish and take care of myself first, but I ended up meeting their needs before mine. All this self-inflicted chaos, stress, and anxiety had worn me down. I made a conscious decision to love me first. To love me more than the attention, meaningless sex, and games I had endured.

I didn't like the person I had become mentally or physically. When I looked in the mirror, my face was round and puffy with scattered acne, extra weight had transformed my curves into bulges of inflamed flesh, my hair was brittle and coming out by the handful every day, and nails bitten all the way down. I was a mess.

I had stopped answering calls and texts, busying myself with overdue projects at home and work. Ghosting them wasn't the most mature way to handle things, but I had my reasons. My year of self-centered relationships had turned into a mess, so the more stressors I eliminated the better. For me, just saying it's over to them was too much. I didn't trust myself not to be wooed by their words and whatever else would drag me back into bed with them.

The weird weight between me and Johnathon had been lifted and we were back to updating each other on our situationships, but less eating, drinking, and smoking for me. I recognized our habits were toxic, but they kept me sane during this attempt to get all three of them out of my system. I was hoping my sessions with Ms. Franklin would help me through this. One thing she kept bringing up was my childhood. I'm guessing my ill-fated choices I made in men had something to do with that. I finally decided to let her in on a little of my past.

"Well, when I was in elementary school, my mom fell on hard times, and I had to go live with my dad. He was married and had a daughter but allowed me to stay anyway. My dad was white from a family that owned a grocery store chain. He was abusive to me, locked me in the closet for whatever. Half of the time I didn't even know what I did wrong. He would say all kinds of hateful shit to me. That closet was the scariest place ever. I felt a demonic presence; there were noises and things or entities touching me. I just knew I was having some type of breakdown when I was locked in that closet. When my mom finally came to get me, I was so happy. But months later, my dad came over, and he and Mom had a fight. She ended up shooting and killing him. In the last few years, I had been having night-mares about everything," I said, numb to what I divulged to Ms. Franklin.

"Wow…that is a lot." For the first time she was speechless.

"Yea, but it was my life," I said with a shoulder shrug.

"I think all that happened has a lot to do with how you handle your relationships now. Being rejected by your dad and witnessing the relationship he had with your mom kind of molded you into the person you are now."

"Maybe." I took a sip of coffee, which immediately made me think of Mike. It had been three weeks since I had talked to or seen him, same with Roy.

"Leesha, this is something we must tackle. Resolving feelings from your past is essential in moving on and mak-ing healthy life and relationship decisions." Ms. Franklin's face wrinkled with concern, which made my chest pang with anxiety. I believed this mess was better left in the past, the nightmares wouldn't kill me, and I already had committed to making better life choices. I would be fine without going down this rabbit hole of emotions. "Our time is almost up, but next session we are going to talk about the time you spent with your father." I was thankful for her warning, part of me thought about canceling the next appointment.

* * *

I made it back to work around 2 p.m. Daniel was at his desk looking disgusted. I didn't even want to know what was going on now, so I pretended not to notice.

"Ms. Roberts, I'm glad you're back," he began. I took a deep breath and let my pen drop. I really didn't want to hear it.

"What's up, Daniel?"

"It's Nancy… one of our residents, Mr. Alberts, complained about hearing her make racial slurs about his daughters after they came to visit him. His daughters complained about some of his clothes that didn't get back from the laundry department. The exchange between them and Nancy got a little heated. After they left, Mr. Alberts overheard Nancy referring to his daughters as *Black bitches*. He was very upset about it and wanted something done about her."

"You have got to be kidding."

I released my tight ponytail to relieve the building pressure in my head and pulled Nancy's file. After a brief review, it was evident this was her pattern. There had been multiple counseling statements with several of them having to do with name calling or racist remarks. I assumed Nancy didn't get fired because she never called into work and was considered a reliable employee. To me, that didn't matter because I knew some staff members called in simply because they didn't want to work with her. She had not only been terrorizing the staff, but now the residents. I called my boss, Mark, hoping he would agree with my intended actions.

After a thirty-minute debate with Mark, I called Nancy into the office. She arrived in regular character; eyes rolling, lips pursed, scoffing at my audacity to call her in.

"I guess you heard about Mr. Alberts and how he and his daughters attacked me over some clothes. I don't even work in the laundry department. What was I supposed to do about it?" She couldn't help but to dig her own grave as she spoke.

"Perhaps get a list and go to laundry and ask about the missing items," I said.

"I did get a list, and I was going to ask them about it." Her nostrils flared as she tightly crossed her arms.

"The complaint is, there was some name calling overheard by the resident involved." I pulled her thick complaint file out, dropping it on my desk so she could see it. Her eyes fluttered as she glanced at the file then at me. "There have been several similar complaints, and you have been counseled about them. Many of these involve racial slurs used by you." After talking to Mark, I didn't have the energy to go back and forth with her, so I got to the point. "We are letting you go. Please get your belongings and leave the premises immediately." She was shocked by the finality in my voice.

"I'm getting a lawyer, and I want copies of that file." She sat there as if she was waiting for me to comply with her demand.

"You may get a lawyer, ma'am, and that lawyer may legally request this file. This file belongs to Lotus Gardens, and it will be released appropriately. Thank you and good-bye." I dismissed her. She got up and opened the office door where a security guard was waiting to escort her.

"You can't be serious!" Her cocky expression quickly turned into embarrassment.

"Oh, I can assure you that I am very serious." I had to get the last word. The security guard led her away. I sat back in my chair, still feeling the heaviness of the day. First the session with Ms. Franklin and then this. I was stressed and drained.

"Wow… that was rare, hardly anyone gets fired here, and you had no problem doing it." Daniel was surprised.

"Now is not the time to procrastinate on things that need to be done, and that was a long time coming." I felt the need to get the things that had been lingering done and getting rid of Nancy was like a huge weight lifted off me at work. Now I wanted to work on building a good relationship with the rest of the staff. This was a great opportunity for a culture change at Lotus Gardens.

"I agree, the change is needed, so let's do it." Daniel's smile was extra big. We spent the remainder of the day re-working the schedule and sending emails out.

I was grateful to have my mind off of my past and the fact I have to reconcile with it sooner than I planned. Actually, I hadn't thought of dealing with it at all. What happened to the idea of letting the past be the past or the cliché, *if you keep looking back you can't move forward?* Why was I even entertaining the thought of dealing with this? I decided not to tackle any of that on my own for now. The only time it would be addressed was with Ms. Franklin, which was all I could handle right now.

A week later, I was still avoiding Mike and Roy. Sporadic knocks on my door, texts, and phone calls were ignored. Avoiding them was difficult; my heart ached. I craved sex, and masturbation wasn't working, it just made things worse. I did a little solo drinking at home to relax at the end of the day, but the alcohol increased my nightmares, so that coping mechanism proved ineffective. Johnathon was out most evenings, so I figured he was seeing someone. He was in a joyful mood every time I saw him. He was never really transparent about his dating life and I was sure he had his reasons.

The sessions with Ms. Franklin continued. I began understanding that fear of rejection kept me from commitment; picking the wrong man was part of my defense mechanism when it came to avoiding relationships. The persistent fear of rejection gifted from my dad was accompanied by the impression I wasn't good enough for anyone. I reluctantly started tackling that mindset.

My goal was to start making better choices, to break the bad habits I had used to numb my emotions and be careful of who I allowed into my life and bed. My year of selfish choices meant for enjoyment and unrestricted pleasure did not go as planned. The only thing that happened was the revealing of open wounds I had secretly carried. The "Lee era" was over. Now it was time for healing and love.

EPILOGUE

At the very least I wanted to become the person I was before Darnell, Mike, Roy, and even Johnathon. I became intentional about caring for my body and mind and began to cultivate healthy habits. I performed a smudging ritual with sage to cleanse the negative energy out of my home and redecorated by changing my comforter to a beige and pink floral design and hung pictures with inspirational quotes in every room. Sweet smelling candles were placed in my kitchen, living room, and bedroom. I added a throw rug underneath the coffee table to give it a more home-like feeling. My apartment finally felt like a sanctuary, a place I didn't mind being alone in and centered around self-love.

My free time was filled with learning to be satisfied with being alone. I purposely limited my time with Johnathon to avoid the self-induced emotional rollercoaster. I also got the tattoo I had wanted forever; a cross on my left thigh wrapped in a vine of flowers that extended through my back around to my right shoulder. It symbolized using faith to bloom into something beautiful.

Ms. Franklin re-enforced what I already knew—that I was more than a man's stress reliever and not just here for the sexual and emotional gratification of others. There was so much more to me than just the spread of my legs or "the happy place in between my thighs." I was a deeply flawed, wonderfully complex human being that actually deserved love… the love from myself.

However, this desired change wasn't without challenges, there was still a tug of war between my mind and my body. I had mentally left the door open for Mike and Roy by not telling them it was over, which allowed me not to commit to the finality of my decision. Deep down I knew my new-found self-assurance would only continue to thrive if Mike and Roy's attempts to contact me ceased. The temptation and fear of creeping back to my old ways constantly lingered, and the longing for attention and validation was ever present. I prayed not to slip back into my old self and to maintain those boundaries. Although I had faith in myself, only time would tell if the strong, self-loving version of Leesha Renée Roberts would endure.

Thank you for reading, The Year of Lee.

Follow Leesha's journey with the next
installment of the Lee Series

BUY NOW

LETTER FROM THE AUTHOR

Thank you for reading The Year of Lee. This is a candid look into Leesha Roberts' self-indulgent phase of casual relationships. This story quickly turns into a cautionary tale of what happens when the emotions take over.

Leesha cultivates relationships with men who are equally self-absorbed in their own ways. If you read carefully, you will find that each man has characteristics that she also possesses, acting as a mirror for her.

We all can relate to at least one of the relationships and understand her emotion-based actions. It's natural to think our decisions and actions would be better, and we could easily avoid the toxic mistakes she made. But mistakes and experiences teach us valuable lessons we otherwise would have never learned. Good and bad, relationships serve as the most important life lessons.

Personal relationships are not the only teachers. Leesha's professional life is an unadulterated example of what Black women encounter in the workplace. Having competence questioned and authority undermined are just small examples of what Black women endure on the job. Many of us can relate to the trauma that goes along with simply trying to function at work. Witnessing Leesha courageously face those challenges also serves as relatable examples and offer encouragement to those in the same position.

It is my hope that you embrace Leesha's imperfections and learn from her mistakes. I also hope you fearlessly experience life, regardless of how messy it gets. Thank you for reading and I hope you continue with Lee's journey.